Touched By Flames

Hidden Realms of Silver Lake
Book 7

Vella Day

Infected with dark magic, this white lighter has to fight for her life.

After being held captive for five months, Danita Warren still has evil blooming inside her—and that scares her more than being in prison. Once she is rescued, Griffin Caspian, the most amazingly kind, protective, and super hot dragon shifter decides he wants to protect her. How lucky could she get? The man is hot. The problem? She doesn't want to drag him down the same dark path.

From the moment Griffin meets Danita, he pledges to devote his life to helping her. Sure, she's his mate, but until she's ready to commit, they can't be together.

Confused as to how to win her heart, he decides that if he can find her missing cousin, she just might want to be with him. And if he can't? He could be doomed forever.

Chapter One

"ARE YOU STILL having nightmares?" Danita Warren's therapist asked.

Why did Dr. Aminor always insist on digging into that wound? There were more pressing things to discuss with her therapist.

Danita rubbed the worn wooden chair arm in the doctor's rather dark office. "Yes. Every night like clockwork."

Her brows rose as she leaned forward. "And? Are they less scary, more scary, longer or shorter in duration than when they first started?"

Danita huffed, hating herself for being so weak. "Ever since that terrible wolf attacked me a few days ago, they have been worse. The strange part is that I don't see his red eyes staring down at me like I would have thought, but rather Sanditra's eyes." Sanditra—that horrible dark lighter who tried to turn Danita's light into darkness.

"Knowing she is dead doesn't seem to help, does it?" her therapist asked as she made a note on her tablet.

"No."

"Why is that, do you suppose?"

"Because I am partially evil. She altered the light inside me when she made me do those despicable acts."

Dr. Aminor added something to her notes. "And why do you think you are evil? Have you done bad things?"

"Not yet, but I can feel some kind of darkness welling up inside me at random times." Danita looked up. "I had a premonition recently—something that has never happened before."

Her doctor's eyes sparkled with interest. "A premonition? This is new. What was it about?"

Danita blew out a breath. "After my recent wolf attack, this woman, Greer Caspian, helped heal my wounds. It was a few days later that I pictured her in trouble. When I told her brother about it, he charged out and was able to save her."

Her therapist smiled. "That sounds like a good thing. You helped save the woman who helped you! I wouldn't call that being dark at all."

"You might think so, but my insides felt as if they were on fire, and I'm not sure why."

"I wouldn't worry about you being evil until you start doing bad things. Helping someone else shows that your white light is still strong."

"I hope so."

"Tell me again about this recurring nightmare."

"Why? It's always the same—Sanditra making me do evil things."

Dr. Aminor waved her stylus at Danita. "Yes, but you remember something different each time. I think when we have all of the pieces, we'll be able to make more sense of it."

Danita doubted that, but she'd try to recall what last night's dream was about. "One minute I'm in my usual cell in the Royal castle, the handcuffs sending poison through my body, and the next I am outside in the dark."

"Then what happens?"

"Sanditra is looming over me with that insidious smile of hers that cuts me to the core. I swear that dark lighter bitch could always see right through me." Danita huffed. "She starts off being nice and then turns really cruel."

"During this dream, you don't know in your heart that she is dead?"

"I don't recall. It's probably because I know she is too evil to be gone for good."

"We've talked about this, you know."

Danita blew out another breath, not appreciating Dr. Aminor's slightly condescending tone. It didn't matter if she was trying to be helpful or not. "I know."

"Did Sanditra force you to perform dark magic last night in your dream?"

"Surprisingly, no. She came, laughed uncontrollably for a minute, and then just left. It was strange."

"How did that make you feel?"

Danita wanted to lash out at the therapist for asking that way too obvious question. "Scared the white light right out of my body." Fear had actually paralyzed her to the point where she couldn't move, not even while asleep.

"Then what happened?"

Danita clenched her fists to keep them from shaking. "Malevolent thoughts bombarded me."

"What did you want to do?" Dr. Aminor asked, her words metered.

"Kill someone. And before you ask who, I don't know, but I suspect it was some Royal for taking me. Then again, it could have been Sanditra for ruining me. I woke up in a sweat, my body trembling and my heart racing."

"You were scared."

Why did she have to state the obvious? "Yes. I'd never had that exact dream before—or those horrible feelings of such rage."

"What did you do to compensate for these evil thoughts?" the doctor asked.

"What you suggested. I pictured myself before I had been kidnapped by the Royals." Danita closed her eyes and entered that pleasant sphere right then. "My safe place is on top of this hill where the pink, yellow, and white wild flowers abound. I imagine being on my back, staring up at the bright blue sky, watching the clouds float by and listening to the birds go about their business. The scene calms me and brings out my light." She reopened her eyes.

Dr. Aminor was actually smiling. "Excellent. Keep doing that."

Just as quickly she sobered. "I think this recent werewolf attack has set you back."

She shook her head. "The attack was painful, sure, but Greer healed me rather quickly. I think it's because I'm still upset over my cousin's recent disappearance that I have these nightly panic attacks. Every time I think about where Wendy could be, extra dark feelings emerge."

"That's maybe why you've been picturing yourself with Sanditra during the night. The darkness could represent your feeling of helplessness."

Way to make me feel worse! "It would seem so."

"There hasn't been any progress on learning Wendy's whereabouts?"

Danita's stomach churned at not only the possibility of losing her beloved cousin and friend, but at losing control over her own thoughts. "No. Nothing."

Dr. Aminor scribbled something on her tablet. "It has to be hard, but you can fight through it. How are you handling these feelings of despair? Besides coming here, of course or picturing yourself on top of a mountain in a field of flowers?"

"I try to think positive thoughts as much as I can, but I fail miserably most of the time. To be honest, I'm increasingly angry with each passing day. That wolf attack was just the final straw I think. Anyone would be upset if her only relative had gone missing. I believe what would help me the most is doing something to find her. Clearly, the police have failed. It's been over a week since Wendy disappeared."

"Danita, please. We've spoken about this. If your cousin was abducted, you need to leave it to the authorities to find her."

Danita's lip uncontrollably curled. "They haven't done a damned thing! A week is a long time to be held captive. I should know!" She was almost shouting.

"Calm down. This isn't helping to bring back the rest of your white light."

It was the reason why she was in therapy in the first place. "I know, but it's so frustrating. Wendy is the only family I have. She's sweet. Kind. This never should have happened to her. What could anyone want with her?"

"Tell me what you do know."

Facts helped to center her, and Dr. Aminor knew that. "Nothing more than what I told the cops and Griffin Caspian." Ah, Griffin. He'd been the one she'd called after that terrible wolf attack in the woods. Within minutes, he was by her side, flying her to safety. He'd also been the one who had helped her after her escape from the Royal prison. She wouldn't have recovered this much if it hadn't been for him. "Wendy's downstairs neighbor heard a commotion in the apartment above hers. Normally, my cousin is super quiet since she works on her articles during the day. She's a journalist. At first, the neighbor thought Wendy was moving furniture, but then she heard a shout followed by a thud. The neighbor is elderly and wasn't about to run to the rescue, so she went next door to speak to her neighbor—only he wasn't home. She returned inside and called the police."

"What did they find?"

"A lamp had been turned over, and a shattered coffee cup was on the floor," Danita said. "Two pillows were also slashed. That seemed rather random to me, but I think they were trying to make it look like a robbery."

"And Wendy?"

"She was nowhere to be found."

"It appears as if she put up a good fight."

"Wendy is a wolf shifter, so I'm hoping she did some damage to her kidnapper." It was the only scenario that made sense.

"Has there been a ransom note or contact of any kind?" Dr. Aminor asked very matter-of-factly.

She shook her head. "Wendy has little money, and she and her dad are estranged. He has no money either, so I don't think this was motivated by greed."

"Then what?"

"I wish I knew," Danita said.

"To help with your feelings of helplessness, you said you wanted to do something. What do you think your options are—other than interfering in a police investigation?"

"I'm not a detective. I'd have no idea where to start."

"Hmm. I suggest you focus on thinking cleansing and positive thoughts then."

Dr. Aminor was no help. "It's hard to do that when I'm so worried about her. I know what captivity can do to a person." Danita refused to think that her cousin was dead though. That negativity could prove lethal to her own soul.

"We talked about this. Negative thoughts are a feeding ground for your dark light to take over your body."

"I know." Damn Sanditra. Before the Royals had kidnapped her, Danita didn't have an ounce of darkness in her. After being held captive for a few weeks by the very powerful dark witch, her white light had started to dim. What she wouldn't give to be like her old self again.

"Understandably, you are angry and anxious," her therapist said, "but in your current mental state, you might do something rash that could make things worse. What if Wendy's kidnapper took you too?"

She shrugged. "I'd at least be with Wendy."

"Danita."

She held up her hands. "Fine. I'll let the police handle things." For now. Besides, Griffin said he would look into it.

"Good. This week I want you to focus only on positive thinking. With a clear head, you might be able to figure out a way to help your cousin."

She doubted that, but it was worth a try. Danita stood, though not any calmer than before she'd walked in, but after her Royal incarceration, she had promised Griffin that she would attend therapy. Just when she'd thought she was ready to embrace the world, her cousin had been kidnapped, and Danita was attacked. No doubt about it, she was cursed. "Thanks, Doc."

In need of a caffeine boost and a snack, Danita decided to walk over to Angelique's café instead of driving there. After being cooped up in that office for an hour, she needed the exercise and fresh air. Too bad it wasn't as cathartic as she'd hoped. Horns made more noise than usual, people seemed pushier, and the wind was whipping her hair into her face and annoying her. For a moment, she was tempted to slow down the world around her to help calm her mind.

But she'd promised herself not to use her magic in that way. While it only took a sweep of a hand and a silent chant, it would take more energy than she possessed right now. It also wouldn't be of any benefit to anyone. Using her powers for her own personal gain would only serve to foster her darkness, which was the last thing she wanted or needed. Ugh.

As soon as she entered the coffee shop though, her negative vibes diminished. Angelique, the restaurant owner, possessed a very powerful white light aura that affected everyone who entered. Her coffee shop was safe, giving Danita a small sense of control.

After ordering a drink and a snack, she snagged a table near the back, needing peace and quiet to think about her next move—a move that Dr. Aminor might not approve of.

Chapter Two

G RIFFIN CASPIAN'S CELL rang. It was his cousin Declan. While Griffin was in charge of sales and trade for Caspian mines, Declan Sinclair was the head of both the Sinclair's and Caspian's mines, which technically made Declan his boss. Thankfully, his cousin always treated him as an equal.

"Hey, what's up?" Griffin asked.

"Are you at the Caspian office today?"

"Yes. I've moved over here. It's quieter than at the SinCas building. Logan and Stone are here too."

"Good. Anderson called and said the man we captured who had kidnapped those shifters and then held them captive in that cave a few months ago, is now willing to talk—but only to us—or rather only to anyone who was in the cave that day. Anderson tried contacting Thane, but he was running drills. Our cousin apparently didn't want to bother Finn, so I guess we're it."

His pulse soared. "Five months is a long time to keep quiet. Why talk now?"

It had been a nightmare when Declan's mate Chelsea had uncovered a potential slave ring of shifters. Even though they'd tried to find the person behind this horrible violation, they had failed. It still stuck in Griffin's craw even after all this time. The Guardians had run into one dead end after another—something that rarely happened.

"We'll have to ask him. You free to do a little interrogating?"

For the first time since the wolf attack on Danita, a rush of energy filled him. It was bad enough he'd made no progress on the disappearance of her cousin Wendy. As a Guardian, helping others was woven into the fabric of his being. While he loved his job at the mine, it was facing and defeating the enemy that really gave him pleasure.

He grabbed the keys to his office. "I'm on my way to the station."

Declan was waiting for him in front of their cousin's desk in the Avonbelle Province Police department.

Griffin nodded to Declan. "Thanks for calling me. I can't believe we're about to get a breakthrough in the case."

"I can't believe it either," Declan said.

Griffin faced his cousin, Detective Anderson Caspian. "Did our human trafficker say why he had a change of heart?"

The man they'd found in the cave with the caged animals had clammed up on the spot and refused to offer any information, despite offering him a deal. Griffin had always suspected that whoever was in charge of the operation was probably holding something over this man's head.

Anderson leaned back in his chair. "Your theory was right. From what I can tell, Gonzalez is just a low-level patsy. He's no hardened criminal. I think these past few months in prison have given him a new perspective, shall we say. He knows he did wrong and wants to repent."

Griffin chuckled. "That, or the thought of spending years and years in prison scares the shit out of him. That's no place for someone like this thin, weak-looking human."

"Regardless of his reasoning, he's now willing to give us some information in order to get a deal."

"I'm willing to listen," Declan said. "We caught him redhanded, so he got what he deserved. I hope he knows that even if he gives us a name now, there is no guarantee that the judge will take any time off his sentence."

"I explained that to him," Anderson said. "But it is equally possible that if he tells us who ordered these men to be captured, the judge might reduce his sentence by a few years."

"In either case, it's win-win for us," Griffin added. "It might even provide some closure for the captured men."

Lucky for this human, the prisons were segregated: shifters in one and humans in another. Even though a human was with his own kind, it was still highly dangerous on the inside. Gonzalez had already been taught a few hard lessons—or so Anderson had said.

Griffin and Declan had saved the ten men, however a couple of townsfolk had come forward claiming someone they knew was also missing. Griffin, Declan, and many of the other Guardians had searched for them but had come up empty-handed. Whether there was any connection to the captive men was anyone's guess.

"Ready?" Declan asked Griffin.

"Let's do this."

Anderson led the way down a dimly lit hallway. When they reached Interrogation Room 3, he opened the door and motioned them in, saying it would be better if he remained outside, probably because the man refused to talk with any cop.

The sorry sack was shackled to the scarred wooden table. Gonzalez looked up, and from the sag in his shoulders, he almost seemed relieved to see them.

Two chairs had been placed across from him. Both Griffin and Declan sat down. "Why the change of heart after all this time?" Declan asked, coming right to the point.

"Malpan threatened me and my family if I said anything. When my wife came by the prison yesterday, she said she'd had enough and was leaving me. I can't say that I blame her. She's been through a lot." Gonzalez buried his head in his hands. "I want that bastard taken down. I don't care what happens to me." He looked up, his jaw now tight.

"Malpan? As in Gregory Malpan, the owner of the copper mine?" Declan asked.

"Yes. This isn't the first time I've worked with that ass either, but he pays really well."

Fury raced through Griffin. "Are you saying you delivered other shifters besides the men we found?" Griffin asked.

Gonzalez held up his hands. "Yes, but I swear to the heavens that until you guys showed up and told me our captives were shifters, I had no idea the animals were really men. I never would have taken shifters. They're humans."

"Not buying it," Griffin said.

"It's the truth," the man stated with a fair amount of conviction.

"Fine. I'll rephrase my question. How many other *animals* did you deliver to Malpan before we caught you red-handed?"

The man looked away. "When you found us in that cave, I was on my third run. The first group consisted of twenty animals, the second fifteen. The last group, as you know, only had ten."

Shit. That meant thirty-five men, and possibly women, were being held somewhere and had been for months. Griffin didn't like this man, but he did seem to be telling the truth. "If you want a chance at a reduced sentence, you will have to give us something concrete. Just saying that Gregory Malpan is a human trafficker or that he threatened your family isn't good enough."

Gonzalez worried his fingers. "I don't know what kind of proof I can give you. I wasn't the one who dealt directly with him."

Likely story.

"Then who did?" Declan asked.

"The two men who owned the animal shelter on the edge of town—Stick and Marty. As I said, I just did what I was told."

"It's rather convenient that they are dead." Too bad Declan had killed both of them five months ago, or he would have dragged the answers out of them.

Gonzalez's face brightened. "They are? Never mind. I did over-hear Marty talking with Malpan on the phone about a second Malpan mine though. I think maybe that's where he might be keeping these animals—I mean shifters."

The idea there were two mines made little sense though. The Guardians surely would have heard if another mine was operating in the vicinity. "Using them for what? Slave labor?"

Gonzalez shrugged. "I don't know. I swear. Look, if you can't put in a good word with the judge, can you at least watch out for my wife—or rather my soon-to-be ex-wife and kid? If Malpan finds out I've talked, he'll send someone after me and them too. I still love her, even if she doesn't want to be with me."

The man's plea rang true. "We'll see what we can do to protect your family."

"Thank you."

Declan pushed back his chair. "If you remember anything else, tell Detective Caspian. He'll contact us."

"Sure, but it's all I know."

Once they stepped into the hallway, Declan faced him. "What are you thinking?"

Griffin could smell a lie from afar. "Other than the fact he claims he didn't know his captives were more than mere animals, I believe him. Malpan probably is threatening his family. Did you see how Gonzalez's hands were shaking, and he didn't shift his gaze when he told us about the other men."

"You might be right. I have to say I didn't expect Malpan to be involved in any of this," Declan said.

"Me neither. To think he used to be a reasonable man," Griffin said.

"Used to be?"

"Don't you remember that his son committed suicide? Ever since then he's been bitter."

"I might be too."

"That's no reason to take it out on others though."

Declan slapped him on his back, but it held no cheer. "I couldn't agree more."

After they all discussed Anderson's next move, Declan and Griffin decided to walk back to the SinCas building, partly to have time to brainstorm. "With the men who ran the animal shelter dead, and Gonzalez not knowing much, where do we go from here?" Griffin asked.

"I'm thinking we need to find that second mine."

"I agree, but Tarradon is a big place. Even if we assume it's in Avonbelle Province, that's a lot of space to cover," Griffin said, his fists clenching.

"We can't let that stop us. Those thirty or so people need to be rescued. Being held prisoner for months on end will destroy even the strongest person."

"I hope there aren't more out there, though who's to say that Malpan—if he is the one guilty of this—hasn't been adding more to his slave trade using another source. It's been more than five months since he received the last batch. Shit. It's possible, he could have sold most of them by now, assuming that was his end game."

Declan snapped his fingers. "Wait a minute. Sanditra was involved in keeping these people in those collars. Remember how she put one around Chelsea's neck when Sanditra captured her?"

"Sure."

"It almost makes it seem as if the dark lighter was the one in charge and not Malpan," Declan said.

"She might have been, but she's been dead for months. Surely her curse would have worn off by now, which makes me wonder why these people haven't escaped. They wouldn't be zombies any longer like that group of ten we found."

Declan blew out a breath. "Your logic is sound, unless Malpan found another dark lighter to take Sanditra's place."

"Shit." Griffin sighed. They turned left toward their destination.

"It's cases like these that are going to turn my red scales gray. Speaking of dead-end cases, any leads on Danita's cousin's disappearance?" Declan asked.

"None. I've spoken to all of the neighbors, but it's like she disappeared into thin air."

"How is Danita holding up? I know those two were close."

"I'll see her tonight, but from what I can tell, she's becoming angrier and more despondent with each passing day," Griffin said.

"After the Changeling attacked her in the woods, she seems to have withdrawn even more. I don't know what to do."

Declan clasped his shoulder and squeezed. "I'm sorry, not only for Danita but for you too."

Griffin had confided in Declan that Danita was his mate, but so far, he'd been unable to get much of a response out of her. He'd decided not to push her since she was dealing with one tragedy after another.

They headed to the elevator, ready to tackle the day. Griffin needed to come up with a plan to find Wendy soon or Danita might never recover.

Chapter Three

DANITA SHOULDN'T BE nervous that Griffin was stopping over tonight, but she was. He'd called earlier to say he wanted to come by to make sure she was doing okay. Physically, she'd healed from the wolf attack, and while she should tell him not to bother looking in on her, she couldn't bring herself to do it. Being around Griffin brought her comfort.

But just like the last few times he'd stopped over, she would tell him everything was fine, and yet somehow he'd worm it out of her that she really wasn't as good as she claimed. He was well aware of just how much her cousin's disappearance was weighing on her.

The problem with tonight's visit was that she was determined to find a way to locate her cousin, and Griffin would not be pleased with her decision to meddle. For her own mental health, she wanted to be a participant instead of merely watching on the sideline. He'd balk at the idea for sure that she wanted to help, which meant she might have to demonstrate a few of her white lighter talents—or maybe they were now dark lighter talents—to prove to him that she was capable of handling herself.

At least when Griffin came over, her white light seemed to shine brighter. It was almost as if she was feeding off of him, drawing out his goodness and taking it for her own. She always worried that she might be affecting him in some negative way, and the last thing she wanted was for her darkness to harm him.

Someone knocked on her apartment door, and she jumped. Jeez. It was only Griffin—or so she hoped. In her old apartment—before she'd been evicted for not paying her rent—she'd had a peephole and a security chain. This dump was lucky it had a door that closed. Griffin had offered many times to find her a better place to live—and even said he'd pay for it—but Danita didn't want to be more beholden to him than she already was. Griffin had then offered to find her a job at SinCas, but she didn't want the charity. She had her pride.

"Who is it?" she asked.

"Griffin."

Her heart sped up until she forced it to calm. Getting her hopes up that they could ever be a couple was juvenile. The two of them couldn't be any more different. She was a white lighter—okay, her time of being able to claim she was one was becoming more suspect with each passing day. Griffin, on the other hand, was this bigger-than-life dragon shifter whose family practically ruled Avonbelle Province. Ever since her escape from the Royal dungeon, she'd only managed to snag a job with a temp agency; hence the reason for living in a dump in the poor end of town. Who would want a woman who had been captured, tortured, and basically had emotional issues?

Griffin Caspian was rich and gorgeous as well as successful. Danita was rather plain, poor, and a failure. Her powers might have returned after his family had sprung her from prison, but the quality and purity of her powers remained suspect.

He's waiting!

Danita pulled open the door and stared—like she often did when she hadn't seen him in a while. Not only was Griffin over six feet five, his muscles had muscles. He'd admitted that working out in the gym was his way of coping with anxious times, but he claimed he didn't focus on building body mass. It just happened.

She thought it cute that his brows were in a perpetual frown, but it was his full lips that were made for kissing that really made her hot. If nothing else, Danita was a pragmatist. Not only was this man way out of her league, but she was too messed up to be thinking about being with anyone—especially a Caspian.

"Hi. Ah, come in."

Why did she become tongue-tied whenever this man came near?

"Hey." He breezed past her, not even studying her this time like he usually did.

She touched his arm to turn him around, but the moment her fingers came in contact with him, her body ignited. Thankfully, a swirl of white light surged, rather than something darker. "Is everything okay?" she asked.

He faced her. "Sort of."

Oh crap. "Did you learn something about Wendy?"

"Wendy? No. This is about those men you helped us locate."

About five months ago, she'd given Griffin and his family a few helpful hints that led them to finding Sanditra—the dark lighter bitch who had nearly destroyed her. That had given them the clue they needed to find ten shifters who'd been held captive in a hidden cave. "What about them?"

Griffin looked around. "I could really use a drink. Would you mind if we head on over to The Wing's Bar where we can talk?"

Danita preferred not being in public. People made her jittery, but he seemed ill at ease at her place, and she couldn't blame him. "Sure."

His brief smile made his face come to life. "Great. Do you want to fly or go by car?" he asked.

Being held in his claws would be too claustrophobic. "Given the choice, I'd prefer not to use your mode of transportation." Yes, he'd carried her after her wolf attack, but she remembered none of it.

He held up a hand. "I'm sorry. I forgot. If I'd been held prisoner, I'd not want to be in anyone's clasp either."

Shit. She'd hurt his feelings, but he did seem to understand. "Let me get my purse."

As soon as she returned with it, Griffin held out his hand for her car keys. She was sure it was because he liked the control, but Danita didn't mind. In fact, she liked having a man take over. Not having to drive gave her more opportunity to keep an eye on the side view mirror. Ever since the Royals had nabbed her, she still feared they would try again. Not to mention, whoever had taken her cousin might come after her too. That was irrational thinking, but Danita couldn't help it.

Thankfully, they arrived at the Wing's Bar in no time. Just as they drew near, someone pulled out of a space in front, and he slid in. Griffin was lucky like that.

He'd asked her to wait for him to open her door, but that only made her more paranoid. He must suspect her life could still be in danger. It didn't seem to matter that Sanditra was now dead.

Her door opened, and he held out his hand to help her out. This time when their fingers touched, she swore his heat shot straight up her arm and pierced her heart. What was wrong with her? Sure, Griffin was hot, intelligent, and intense, but he was also brooding and rather over-the-top protective. Despite his shortcomings, she desired him. Acting on those urges however was something she wouldn't do. Griffin deserved a lot better.

Inside Wings, the noise was surprisingly tolerable. The place smelled of both sweet and tangy beer, and the fairly lively music helped take her mind off being in a public place.

Griffin pressed his palm against her back, once more making her hyper-aware of him. "Let's sit in a booth over there." He nodded to a seat in the corner.

Once they were settled, his cousin Finn came over. His mate had mentioned that Finn bartended there four nights a week.

"Fancy seeing you here, Griff." Finn faced her. "Danita. I'm sorry about the Changeling attack. How are you feeling?"

Griffin gave Finn the stink eye. She looked over at Griffin. "It's okay. I know your family is aware of what happened, and that they are responsible for taking down the red-eyed devil."

"Sorry," Finn said. "You look good."

She smiled. "Thanks."

"What can I get you two?"

Griffin looked over at her, his brows raised. "I'll have a glass of white wine, please," she said. Danita wasn't really in the mood to drink, but she needed the courage to talk to Griffin about finding her cousin.

"An Answalt," Griffin said. Once Finn disappeared, Griffin faced her and inhaled. "I have a favor to ask."

That wasn't what she expected him to say. "What's that?"

"I received some information today about a possible lead on the man responsible for kidnapping the ten shifters."

"That is good news. Did one of the men remember something?"

He shook his head. "I actually spoke with a few of them last week. None of them have remembered what happened even after all this time. They said it's like they are still in a fog."

"A fog? As in a spell is still controlling them?"

"Maybe. One of the men said it was like he'd had his memory erased, and his reason for existing seems to have been damaged."

She shook her head. "I didn't experience anything like that when I was under Sanditra's spell."

Griffin blew out a breath. "I'm happy to hear that. I was actually hoping you knew of a spell that could return them to normal."

"I do have talents, but mine aren't that kind. My range of spells are rather specific. Have you asked Angelique to see if she knows of anyone who can perform something like that?"

"No, but I can contact her." Griffin flashed her another smile, and her pulse beat wildly.

Finn came over with their drinks. "Just holler if you need a refill." He placed her wine in front of her and Griffin's beer in front of him, before rushing back to the bar.

"The captured men have no idea who took them then?" she asked.

With the kidnappers dead or in custody, together with the fact the captured shifters were all men, Danita had no reason to believe Wendy met with the same fate, but she wanted to leave no stone unturned.

"No, but the man who helped kidnap them talked today."

She lifted her wine glass with both hands. "What did he say?" Danita was pleased her tone remained fairly calm. Inside, a swell of darkness was swirling.

Griffin leaned closer. "Arthur Gonzalez claims that Gregory Malpan is the one who captured the shifters."

"Malpan? He's a miner, like you. What would be his end game?"

"I don't know. All I can think of is that he is using these men as slaves in his mine. Nothing else makes sense."

There went her theory about Wendy possibly being among them. She was a strong woman, but Danita saw no benefit in taking a female.

"I find it hard to believe that no one has leaked this horror. I have a friend who works in the Malpan mine, and he would have said something if they used slaves."

"According to Gonzalez, Malpan has a second mine," Griffin said.

Her pulse sped up. "Why don't you go there and expose him then?"

Griffin tossed back a good portion of his beer. "If I knew where this mine was, I would."

"Your family doesn't know where all of the copper veins are located?"

He shook his head. "I wish we did. We certainly can fly around and look for activity, but no telling how long that would take."

A crazy idea struck her. Almost giddy, Danita looked around and leaned forward. "As you know, I work for a temp agency. How about if I ask to be placed in his office? I can snoop from there."

Griffin slapped the table, and the man in the booth behind them turned around. "Absolutely not," he said. "It's too dangerous."

"It's not like they would have me work in the mines."

His eyebrows rose. "You don't know that."

Her stomach flipped. "What aren't you telling me?" He better not be withholding information about Wendy.

"Nothing, but anyone who would capture people and then use a dark lighter to make them forget things, isn't someone you want to be around."

She'd expected he'd say something like that. "It's not like I'm without my own talents to protect myself."

"Are you saying you have some hidden ability to take down an army? Because anything less than that could get you killed."

Griffin was being ridiculous. "No, but I can do spells."

"Will your spell make Malpan tell you where this mine is hidden?"

She'd never tried to make anyone tell the truth before. "Probably not."

"Even you have to admit that it wouldn't be safe for you if he catches you asking too many questions."

She supposed it wouldn't be terrible to show Griffin what she was capable of. "I'd be safe."

"Like you were against that Changeling?"

"I was attacked from behind. I didn't have time to do any spell."

"Malpan may do the same."

She huffed. "I'll be super careful. Are you certain that Malpan is guilty?"

Griffin glanced away. "No, I'm not. I do believe the underling who took these shifters believed he was telling the truth when he said Malpan was in charge."

"Malpan could be guilty, or this man was just trying to get something from you."

"Damn. You might be right." His top lip curled. "I wanted the bastard who did this worse than anything, which meant I might have been desperate for a name." He grunted. "Enslaving someone is as bad as torture."

"How true." She knew first-hand about both. Needing a moment to compose herself, Danita closed her eyes and pictured everything around her moving in slow motion. After she opened them, she waved her hand and focused intensely. To her delight, everything came to a near stop—including Griffin whose hand was half raised. The noise in the room dropped close to silence, and the beer someone was pouring at a table nearby slowed to a trickle.

To prove that she could escape unnoticed, Danita grabbed her purse, slipped out of the booth, and left.

Chapter Four

WHAT THE HELL? Every muscle in Griffin's body locked up. He was talking with Danita a second ago, and now she was gone. Had someone put a spell on him to make him lose his sense of time? He searched the bar area for her, but everything seemed like business as usual, yet Danita wasn't there.

Oh shit. Had someone kidnapped her without his knowledge? Griffin didn't believe that was even possible. Then reason intruded. People would be running around and shouting if some thugs had come in and dragged off a woman. Not to mention, Danita would have gone kicking and screaming.

He slid out of the booth, tossed down some money for the two drinks and ran up to the bar. "Finn!"

His cousin's mate held up a finger, finished pouring a drink for a customer, and then came over. "Need another one?"

"No. Did you see what happened to Danita?" He hated that his pulse was racing, but this was his mate he was talking about. He couldn't let anything happen to her.

"What are you talking about? She's right behind you."

Griffin spun around, unable to comprehend her grin—something he rarely saw on her beautiful face. "Where did you go?" he asked between gritted teeth.

"I stepped outside for a moment."

"How? When?"

She threaded her arm through his and escorted him back to the booth. "I told you I could take care of myself." Her smug attitude confused him. He'd never seen this side of her before.

Once they reached their booth, Danita released his arm and slid onto the seat. She then picked up her half-finished glass of wine and polished it off.

"What exactly happened?" he asked.

"You mean this?" Danita reached across the table and grabbed Griffin's hand. Holding it, she quickly closed her eyes and waved her other hand. As if the world tilted, everything came to a near stop. The music slowed to one low note after another. Someone in the process of sitting down seemed suspended in air. Possibly because she was still connected to him that the slow motion didn't reach him.

In awe, he looked around. She snapped her fingers, and all went back to regular speed. Once more, no one seemed to be aware of what had happened. No shouts or looks of confusion.

"How did you do that?" he asked. It was the most remarkable thing he'd ever seen—and the Four Sisters of Fate had tested his beliefs in reality many times.

"I'm a white lighter."

"So are Kaleena and Tory, and yet neither of them can do that."

"Each white lighter possesses slightly different talents. When I was growing up, I was fascinated with the concept of time. I practiced using telekinesis to move small objects, but it wasn't until recently that I could actually stop movements in an entire room like this." She glanced to the side, acting as if what she was about to tell him wasn't good. "As a kid, I could slow a car down but never a whole group of people like I can now." She clasped her empty glass and held on tight, her nervous energy reaching him.

"Did Sanditra teach you this new trick?"

Her cheeks reddened, and she broke eye contact. "Yes, but don't worry. I won't abuse my power, I swear."

Griffin held up his hands. Danita was such a sweet woman. "It's okay. I wasn't judging. I need to understand what you can do. I like that you can protect yourself though."

She set down her wine glass. "I can, unless I'm overpowered or something. No one is invincible. Not even you, I bet."

Was that a challenge? "I kind of am—invincible that is. Remember, I have my dragon to heal me if I'm attacked." That was part of the reason his kind lived to be hundreds of years old. The aging process moved at a crawl too, giving him a youthful appearance even though he was over one hundred years old.

"There is that. I have no healing powers."

Once they mated—or rather if they mated—she'd have plenty of healing abilities. "My dragon has needed help when my injuries were severe. I'm lucky our family has two of the best healers around."

"Greer and Declan."

"Correct."

She studied him for a moment. "I'm guessing that as a Guardian, you often get into fights?"

"I do when I have to help save a woman from prison."

She leaned back and grinned. Yes, things were looking up. It didn't matter he hadn't been the one to enter the prison and spring her. Lily had those honors.

"So, tell me about this secret life of a protector," she said. Danita leaned forward, clearly wanting to learn more about him.

"Nothing much to tell. Because my family and the Sinclairs own profitable mines, there are always people trying to take away our wealth. I was taught at a young age to fight for what was mine."

"I meant as a Guardian."

"We help where we are needed. That's all."

"I assume you train a lot. I know you said you lift weights."

Griffin should have told her more about himself, but he never had the sense she was interested. He had checked up on her every week or so after her release, but they never went out on dates. He mostly stopped by to make sure she was doing okay and to see how her therapy sessions were going. He'd never fully explained the complete role of the Guardians for fear she'd worry about his safety. "Thane trains us regularly. It's not like we go out looking for fights. We don't like to kill."

"I see."

He finished his beer. "I think I should take you home before you cause anymore shocks to my system."

She laughed, and he wanted to hold and kiss her forever.

DESPITE THE BRIEF shot of pride running through her at impressing Griffin with her skills, Danita's world was still out of control. All during the drive back to her apartment, her mind spun with what she could do to help save the men who'd been captured by Malpan. Obviously, she had no idea how to help find Wendy.

Not only would a good deed go a long way to restoring her white light, and possibly help quell the intensity of her nightmares, she wanted to do something for Griffin. He really seemed intent on finding these men. Goddess only knew, she owed this man her life many times over.

As a side benefit, if she was busy helping to find these men, it might help take her mind off of her cousin's disappearance. If Danita stopped being so focused on Wendy's plight, she might come up with a solution on how to find her.

The big issue she faced now was how to get a job at Malpan Mining without attracting attention. If Malpan caught her snooping around or asking too many questions, she might be able to escape from some uncomfortable situation by slowing down time, but it wasn't like she could hide forever. Luck would have to be on her side.

When they arrived at her place, Griffin cut the engine, and then came over to her side to open her door. Without saying anything, he escorted her into her apartment building. He was probably trying to figure out a polite way of telling her to stay out of his business.

Like that would happen. She had a plan. And a good one that she hoped would work.

Because Danita lived on the second floor, they took the stairs to her apartment. At her place, he spun around to face her. "Promise me one thing."

Here it comes! "What?"

"You won't do anything that could get you into trouble. And by that, I mean, please don't poke a stick at Malpan Mining. It could get you killed." His eyes shimmered, and she swore some of his scales flashed a pretty rust color.

His attitude somehow pissed her off. "I told you I could handle myself."

Not wanting to continue this conversation, she stepped around him and jammed the key in the lock. Thankfully, it opened on the first try, and she stepped inside. Just as she turned around to close it, Griffin entered and loomed over her.

"I know you can handle yourself, but I'd feel responsible if something went wrong."

"You aren't responsible for me. Any incident would be all my fault."

He blew out a breath. "Just be careful, okay? I care about you." His eyes changed from light brown to almost teal.

Before she could ask what was happening, he gently clasped her shoulders, leaned over, and kissed her—rather chastely mind you— but the contact altered something inside her, nonetheless.

A bit breathless, she leaned back. "I'll think about it." She wouldn't change her mind. It wasn't who she was.

"Thank you. Like I said, if anything happened to you…"

Why was he so concerned about her—a nobody? Not only that, her light was turning darker by the moment.

Danita planted a hand on his chest. "I appreciate all you've done for me, but to be honest, I wish everyone would stop telling me what to do." Shit. Her tone had come out a bit too harsh.

He practically jumped back and held up his hands. "I just meant that I like you." He stabbed a hand through his hair. "I'm not trying to tell you how to live your life, Danita. I was merely cautioning you."

He did sound sincere. "I'm sorry. I like you too, but for the last few months my life hasn't exactly been moving in a positive direction. First, I'm kidnapped and then subjected to filth, sickness, pain, and a mental violation so horrible, it was as if someone was ripping out my insides." That wasn't far from the truth. There must have been a hole somewhere on her body because with each passing day more goodness was seeping out of her. The nightmares proved that. "I feel as if I have no control over anything anymore. It's why I want to help you."

Griffin cupped her face. "Then let me help you find your white light."

He was the sweetest man alive. "No one can help me."

She slid out of his grasp, wrapped her arms around her waist, and traipsed over to the ripped chair across from the sofa. She slid down onto the seat and dropped her head in her hands.

Footsteps sounded as Griffin neared. He squatted in front of her and lowered her arms, forcing her to look into his face.

"I didn't tell you the whole truth before," he said. "And you deserve to know."

Her heart dropped to her stomach. A hundred scenarios swam in her brain. She doubted he'd tell her he was married. Hell, with her luck he'd say he was a dark lighter in disguise. Okay, that was a stretch, but anything was possible.

"The truth about what?" She sat back and blew out a breath.

"I'm not sure how to tell you this, but we are mates—fated to be together. It's why I need to protect you."

Danita knew all the stories about shifter love and their belief in the *one and only*. She just didn't buy into that craziness. "What did you do? Pull the short straw?" That wasn't nice, but it provided her with more proof that her dark light was slowly taking over her body.

"How can you say that? We belong together."

"I don't know how to break it to you, fly boy, but you really don't need me in your life. I used to be fine, but trust me, it wouldn't be good for you to be with me right now." She had to save him from herself.

He shook his head. "Let me tell you something." He stood and pulled her to her feet. Griffin walked her the few steps to the sofa, pressed lightly on her shoulders, forcing her to sit, and then sat down next to her.

With him being so close, it made her more vulnerable—a feeling she didn't like. "What is it?" she asked.

"When you were in the Royal prison, Lily, my brother's mate, was determined to save you."

"And she did."

"Yes, but did you realize that she only helped three of you? She left the rest of the prisoners."

Danita had wondered about why she'd done that. "I figured Lily either didn't have time to save more or those who were left belonged there."

One side of his mouth quirked into a half smile. "You're right. She only released the good ones."

"How did she know who was good and who wasn't?" At the time, Danita's darkness had only started to grow.

He glanced off to the side. "I have a friend who is...a white lighter. She actually went to the prison, checked each of you out, and told us who was worthy."

Danita shook her head. "I never saw anyone." Or had this white lighter stopped time like she was able to?

"She teleported and left rather quickly." He waved a hand. "I wasn't there, but my brother Birk told me that was what happened."

He was such a trusting and wonderful man, but he was also a bit naïve. "I might have been pure then, but ever since...not so much."

"I don't believe you."

Danita huffed out a laugh. "Every time I think about Wendy or about the men who are being held captive, I become angry."

"I'm angry too." He seemed to be losing patience with her.

"It's different." Not wanting to look at him, she twisted to the side.

"Danita, don't shut me out. Let me help you."

While it was true that when she was with Griffin, her darkness seemed to weaken, it wasn't fair to him. "Like I said before. You can't help me. No one can. I have to work through this myself."

He scooted closer, turned her toward him, and cupped the back of her head. Then he kissed her again.

Whoa. This kiss was more demanding and passionate than the one before. Talk about heat and excitement. It was almost as if he wanted to prove to her that he'd be there for her no matter what.

And that was the problem.

The more she let him in, the less control she'd have over her thoughts—over her life.

Because of the way her body was reacting to him, she was willing to lose a bit of control. His manly and powerful scent, his strong hands and arms, and his mental strength flowed into her. For the moment, her white light was pushing aside the dark—and she liked it.

As if her hands had a will of their own, she clasped the side of his face to drink him in. Wanting to participate more fully, she parted her lips. When their tongues touched, her nipples hardened, and she yearned for his touch. Tears of joy spilled over her lashes.

Griffin jerked back. "Did I hurt you?"

She sniffled. "No. It was nice. Actually, it was more than nice." For that moment, it was as if time had stood still. The problem was that she'd lost control, and she didn't like it. "I think you should go."

"Seriously?" Griffin asked.

She nodded. "It's better if…" She waved a hand. "Let's leave it at that."

He stood, and she did too. "Sleep well then," Griffin said. His warmth and passion from a moment ago gone.

Without a glance backward, he strode out the door. Damn. Danita was so confused. Mates? Really?

Okay, it would be a dream come true to have someone as handsome, noble, and kind to be with her, but Griffin Caspian deserved a lot better. Yes, for his sake, she needed to stay away from him.

Chapter Five

G RIFFIN HAD NOT slept more than a few winks last night mostly because he couldn't keep his mind off Danita. The woman was remarkable in so many ways yet highly frustrating at the same time. She'd been through a lot and had survived. He admired that. However, a shifter dreamed of the day he told his mate they belonged together, and while Danita's reaction wasn't totally negative, she certainly didn't act excited. That totally confounded him—and upset him—big time.

A small setback wasn't an excuse to become unhinged however. Caspians always persevered, especially in the face of adversity. That meant he would do whatever it took to win her heart. If they had any chance of being together, he needed to figure out a way to rid Danita's body of the darkness she claimed possessed her. The horror of it consuming her seemed to be what was stopping her from furthering their relationship—or so he wanted to believe.

His cousin Declan had been called to Earth to heal a shifter who had a spell put on him by a dark goddess. Unfortunately, it had taken both Declan and another powerful white lighter, Ophelia, to cure the shifter. Damn.

Danita claimed she wanted, or rather needed, control in her life, and his interference was not welcome. Fine. But if she didn't figure things out on her own and soon, he might have to ask for help from the Four Sisters of Fate. Surely, they'd do something. After all, Danita was his mate, and Fate was very important to them.

Or…could it be that Danita was using her white light-dark light issues as an excuse not to mate with him? Was there some other reason she didn't want to be with him that had nothing to do with her problems? Perhaps having the ability to shift into a dragon scared her. But why? Tarradon was full of shifters, especially his kind.

Whatever her reason, she was hiding it from him. Sure, she said her darkness was growing, but he didn't buy it. She cared too much about finding her cousin. Danita Warren was a good person. She also was concerned about the men who were being held captive. Dark lighters were sociopathic and certainly not empathetic.

If he could locate Wendy, perhaps Danita would look more favorably on him. Without the anxiety of having her only relative missing, she might be able to conquer this whole dark-lighter stuff. That was the key for sure: find Wendy.

With a newfound focus, he raced to the roof of his building, shifted, and headed to the Caspian mines. The trip was short but enjoyable. Flying cleared Griffin's head since it gave him time to reflect.

When he spotted the mine below, he landed and then shifted back. During the flight he'd come up with an idea—one that his brother Logan, the computer genius of the family, could help him with. If he could check Wendy's last phone calls, or whatever magic Logan used to locate people, Griffin might be able to find a lead.

Just as he entered the building, Logan stormed out of his office. "I was just coming to look for you," his brother said, his tone hard and his posture stiff.

Hopefully, his piss poor mood had nothing to do with the mines—or Wendy. "What is it?"

"Come into the office, and I'll show you." Griffin said hello to their receptionist and then followed his brother. Once in Logan's office, he pulled up a chair and motioned for Griffin to sit down.

"I was doing the end of the month report and found something I didn't like. Did you see that our copper sales are down by forty percent this month over last?"

Griffin's blood pressure skyrocketed. He hadn't noticed, and it was his job to be on top of those things. "No. I've been busy."

"You're the head of fucking sales. How could you not know?" He stabbed a hand through his hair. "Sorry. I didn't mean to accuse you of anything, but shit, how did this happen?"

This was bad. Logan never lost his cool, and Griffin never shirked his responsibilities. The Guardians counted on him. "Are you sure this is right?"

Logan swung his computer screen to face him. "Numbers don't lie."

Griffin's pulse soared. "No, they don't. I'm not sure how this happened, but I'll delve into it right away."

"You better." Logan huffed out a breath. "I'll dig into it too."

"Thanks."

His mind racing, Griffin stood and trudged back to his office. He was the eldest Caspian, and as such, the weight of the family business fell onto his shoulders. Sure, Declan Sinclair oversaw the running of both mines, but the business end of the Caspian mines fell to him and Logan.

Once in his office down the hall, Griffin booted up his computer and studied the trends. Two months ago, their copper sales had begun to fall, but this past month had been worse. He might have blamed the economy, but the sale of all other metals had risen.

Fuck. While Griffin only had the word of an unscrupulous man that Malpan had slaves working in his secret mine, it might be the reason for the decline. Malpan would be able to produce copper at very little cost if he didn't have to pay for labor.

Griffin tapped a few keys to bring up the copper sales of the past six months. His best client was Ralph Whitmore, a contractor who built high rises and who plumbed with copper. Whitmore had purchased copper weekly from Caspian mines—until three weeks ago. Griffin checked his other clients, and the result was more or less the same. This was worse than he thought possible. He'd let down his family, and his chest pinched tight.

It was definitely time for a little investigation. He needed to be sure that the cause of the bad sales was due to Malpan's illegal activities before he accused the man of unscrupulous practices.

Given Logan's frame of mind, Griffin wasn't going to ask him to do his computer magic on Wendy. Griffin would have to figure things out on his own. Too bad time was running out for the missing girl. Sure, the police were on the search, but according to his cousin Anderson, Wendy had disappeared without a trace.

Griffin was faced with a dilemma. He had to prevent his family's business from going down, and he needed to find Wendy if he had any hope of saving Danita. Taking his focus away from the girl might jeopardize his future with his mate. Not finding the source of the loss could harm his family. Shit.

THE NEXT MORNING Danita stopped by the temporary office where she worked. "Hey, Marie. Do you remember if Malpan Mining has ever asked for an agency member to work for them before?" It was a reasonable question since most companies in town requested a temp for one reason or another. All she'd need was a few days to snoop.

"Why that company? You've never asked about a specific place before," her boss said.

Lying went against her nature, but Danita's need for control grew each day. If she could help Griffin and those men, it might keep the darkness at bay. "I heard it was really nice there. I have a friend who works in the mine, and he says the conditions there are good."

Her boss lowered her chin and raised her brows, a small smile creeping up her face. "Someone of interest per chance?"

Marie had been harping on Danita to find someone to date. She preached that sex cured all mental ills. If Danita indulged in that activity, it wouldn't be with her friend at the mine. She liked Griffin too much.

"Maybe."

Her smile broadened. "Let me give them a call."

Danita waited in the main room while Marie ducked into her office. She returned a few minutes later. "Sorry. They have no openings, but I found something else you might be interested in."

It would be impolite not to ask where. "Oh, what is it?"

"Have you ever picked berries at a farm?"

She couldn't afford to be sidetracked. "No, but I strained my back the other day." She rubbed the theoretically sore area for effect. Darkness from that lie swirled inside her, and Danita hoped it didn't reflect on her face. "That's okay. I appreciate you checking for me. I'm sure a job will come up soon."

"It always does."

Once outside, Danita had no choice but to head to Malpan Mining. She had a plan, but it would cost her dearly to follow through. First though, she needed to pick up something from her apartment. It wasn't often that she did spells, but ever since attending the sessions with Dr. Aminor, she'd been practicing. Only this time, the spell she planned to use wouldn't be sanctioned by any therapist.

GRIFFIN CONGRATULATED HIMSELF on keeping his cool, especially when speaking with Caspian Mines' best copper purchaser, Ralph Whitmore. He'd wanted to shake the man and ask him whether good service and high quality counted for something. After all, Griffin had been giving Whitmore discounts for years.

It took all of Griffin's control not to tell Whitmore that Malpan was able to provide him with such great prices because the miner was using slaves. Without proof though, Griffin couldn't shout his suspicions to the world. He could only hope that when the former clients of Caspian mines learned the truth about Malpan that they'd start buying from him again.

Once Griffin finished his discussions with his former clients, he was so frustrated that he desperately needed a break. The only people who had ever been able to help him and the rest of the Guardians were the Four Sisters, so he headed to their pottery shop. Griffin's visit was not to request interference for Danita and her dark lighter issues, but to see if they knew anything about these men being held captive in Malpan's mine.

It was during work hours, so there might be customers at the shop, which meant he'd have to be patient if the sisters weren't alone. When he entered their store, sure enough, Poppy, as well as a pregnant Magnolia, were each with a customer. The sisters smiled and waved to him before returning to their clients.

While he waited, Griffin walked around the shop. In the times he'd had to confer with these white lighters about some emergency, his mind hadn't been on the pottery. This time he studied their art. It was quite sensational, really. Besides the usual cups and plates, there were trinkets, if that was even the right word for them. One piece in particular spoke to him. It was a figurine of a woman kneeling among a bed of flowers looking up at the sky. It reminded him of Danita. Like his mate, she had shoulder length dark hair and beautiful light hazel eyes. It was almost as if this piece were alive.

"It's lifelike, isn't it?" said a female voice behind him.

Griffin spun around, the figurine still in his hands. "Yes. It's quite remarkable."

Poppy smiled. "Does it remind you of someone?"

Could this woman read minds? He wouldn't put it past her. The Four Sisters had many talents, few of which he or any other Guardian understood. "Very much so. I'd like to buy it."

"Wonderful. I can check you out at the counter."

While he paid, he decided now was a good time to bring up his concern. "I'm hoping you can help me with something."

She inhaled deeply. "Is Danita in trouble?"

His jaw slightly dropped. Griffin had never mentioned his mate's name. "No, but how did you know about her?"

Poppy tapped her head and smiled. "Really?"

Griffin didn't know why he was surprised. "Sorry. This isn't about Danita, so maybe you can't help. Do you remember the shifters that were being held captive in the cave and who were forced to wear poisonous collars?" Poppy and Magnolia had helped remove the offending cuffs.

"Of course. I was led to believe they had survived."

"They did, but their minds are still foggy about what happened. But that's not why I've come. From what I've been told, there were many more like them out there. The man who helped capture them said that Gregory Malpan was responsible for this offense. From what Gonzalez understood, these men were sent to a mine to be used as slaves."

"Oh, my. That's terrible. What can I do to help?"

"Is there any way you can help me find this mine?"

Poppy looked over her shoulder. Magnolia wasn't with a customer any longer and was straightening some items on a shelf. "Let me speak with my sister. This is not in our usual wheelhouse."

Poppy closed her eyes. When Griffin glanced over, her sister's were closed as well. He assumed they were conversing telepathically, something a shifter could only do with his mate. Griffin needed to ask Danita if she had the ability to do this with other white lighters. His cousins Kaleena and Tory never claimed to be so inclined, but maybe that wasn't part of their abilities.

Poppy's eyes opened. "I'm afraid there is nothing we can do. Since your mate is not in danger, our hands are tied. But don't worry, you and Danita are on a path that Fate has set. Looking for Malpan is the right course."

He figured they'd say that, but he had to try. "Thank you anyway." Damn.

At least he found a present for Danita, and Poppy confirmed that he needed to deal with Malpan.

Dejected at not learning the precise location of this secret mine, he headed back to work. He needed to do a little brainstorming with Logan, assuming his brother wasn't still royally pissed at him for screwing up. He hoped that when he explained who'd stolen their clients away, Logan would understand. Clearly, if they didn't stop Malpan, not only would they lose copper sales, men's lives would be ruined.

Chapter Six

BECAUSE DANITA'S TEMPORARY agency didn't have any useful jobs for her today—other than picking fruit—she decided to take things into her own hands. Her plan? Apply for a real job at Malpan Mining for a few days in the hopes of learning where this extra mine was located. If Malpan was keeping slaves, surely someone would let something slip. A hired hand had to be assigned to watch them at night and take them food during the day. Right?

Not only that, the slaves had to sleep somewhere. Were they escorted to another facility, or were the men told to shift at night and then chained up like animals, making it harder to find them? A shiver raced through her at that reminder of being held captive and treated like an animal herself.

Once she arrived at the main mine entrance, Danita checked her rearview mirror to make sure she looked presentable. If she was told there was no opening, then she'd plant her small bag of herbs in the receptionist's desk. Together with a well-placed curse, the secretary would not be coming in tomorrow. Hello, temp agency phone call.

She almost laughed at the simplicity. The secretary would recover just as soon as Danita removed the spell. Its ease was brilliant and safe.

Wanting to appear desperate, she lowered her gaze as she entered the building. The office wasn't as large as she'd expected, nor was it well maintained. The walls needed a fresh coat of paint, and none of the paintings on the walls matched in style. The receptionist sat behind a waist high counter that was situated in the middle of the small room.

The young blonde looked up and smiled. "Can I help you?"

"I was wondering if you were hiring?" Danita cleared her throat. "I recently lost my job as an accountant and am trying to find work. I'll take anything: cleaning, answering phones, whatever. Even if it's only for a few days I would appreciate it. I really need the money."

The receptionist tilted her head and pressed her lips together in sympathy. "I am so sorry. This is a small company. Unless you can work in the mines or drive a truck, there's only me and Mr. Malpan in the office."

Damn. Danita had no choice then. She closed her eyes and said a silent chant as she waved her hand to stop motion. She hadn't planned to use this talent so soon, but the tall counter threw her off balance since it wasn't obvious where she could put the herbs. Once the woman's movements basically halted, Danita rushed to the other side of the counter, pulled open a drawer and slipped the herbal packet under some papers. After returning to the other side of the counter, she waved her hand again, returning the receptionist to her former animated state.

Danita dipped her head. "Darn. Well, thanks anyway."

With her mission accomplished, Danita hurried outside. It wasn't until she was almost home that the enormity of what she'd done hit her. She'd put an evil spell on a very nice person. While the young girl would have a few uncomfortable days, how dark was Danita willing to go to recover her white light? And was it even possible to use evil to banish evil?

Once back in town, Danita stopped at Angelique's café hoping to speak with the owner, a wonderful white lighter who seemed to possess all kinds of answers. Danita ordered a coffee with a topping of whipped cream—something she only did under high stress situations—and today certainly qualified.

As if Angelique could sense her, she exited the kitchen and stepped in front of her. "Danita! Nice to see you back here so soon."

Usually, Danita only stopped in once a week, but this was the second time in three days. "Can we talk?"

"Sure. Let me deliver these drinks. Have a seat."

Danita paid for the drink she ordered and headed over to a booth. She set the order number in front of her and looked around. Fortunately, she didn't spot anyone she knew. Having an idle conversation right now would be difficult.

Angelique slid in across from her. "What's up?"

Danita sighed. "You know how I told you that I'm having a hard time keeping my darkness from taking over the light?"

"Yes, but I thought you were working on positive spells."

"I was until I learned about the possible location of those extra shifters that Sanditra put an evil spell on." Angelique had been instrumental in taking down that dark lighter.

"After all this time, you know where they are?"

"Not yet."

She explained what Griffin had told her about Gregory Malpan possibly being responsible for the men's capture. Danita had asked Angelique if she could help find Wendy when she first learned of her cousin's disappearance, but so far Angelique hadn't had any luck. Asking to help with the men might put a strain on their relationship, but Danita was desperate.

"I was hoping you could ask around and see if anyone knows where this mine might be located." Even though Angelique hadn't been in town all that long, she seemed to have deep and powerful connections. Hell, in one afternoon, she'd found out where Sanditra was holding Declan's mate captive.

"People I can find sometimes, but mines? I don't think so."

"I understand." Danita blew out a breath. "I came to ask you something else too."

"Anything."

"You know the saying that the ends justify the means?"

Angelique chuckled. "And those means are dark, and the end represents the light, right?"

How did she know what Danita was thinking? "Yes. I thought I'd go undercover for a few days at Malpan Mining to see if I could learn something, but they didn't have an opening since they are a small operation."

"And you decided to use some of your residual dark magic to provide that opening."

Was she that transparent? "Yes. Now I feel bad about it. Using dark to help provide me with light doesn't seem right."

"That's because it's not. You know what you have to do."

Her shoulders sagged. "Stop doing bad spells, but I can't seem to prevent myself. It's becoming an addiction."

"That's always how it starts."

Danita's pulse raced. "The problem is that I want these men freed! My therapist thinks that if I can provide some good in this world, my darkness will diminish, giving me more control over my thoughts. More control means clearer thinking. And if I can think more clearly, I can figure out a way to help Wendy."

"Ah. I see the strange logic." Angelique leaned back in her seat. "You have to do what you think is right."

She said the words Danita wanted to hear, but she had the sense Angelique still didn't approve.

"I wouldn't have put the rather mild spell on the secretary, but my nightmares are becoming increasingly more disturbing. I'm spiraling out of control."

"I hate seeing you in such pain. What are these nightmares about?" Angelique asked.

She sounded like Dr. Aminor. "Last night, it was about Malpan. I dreamed I had my hands around his neck, strangling him. I know I'm not strong enough to kill him, but my subconscious wanted him dead."

"I hope you find out the location of this secret mine before you actually do end his life."

Angelique's fairly ridiculous statement made Danita see how stressed out she really was. "I'm not homicidal. Yet."

A waitress carried over her order and placed it in front of her. Danita lifted the lid and watched the steam pour off the top.

"Have you spoken to Griffin about your…plans?" Angelique asked.

Instantly, Danita's stomach coiled. "No. He'd probably lock me in a room and throw away the key if he learned what I was planning."

"If it's that dangerous, why do it?"

Danita tossed her a small smile. "Like you, I have some talents. I can take care of myself."

"Just be careful." Angelique glanced toward the service area where someone was waving to her.

"Don't worry. I will be."

Angelique said her goodbyes and returned to work. Once Danita finished her drink, and in need of some reflection, she decided to take a drive to her favorite spot.

Once she arrived at the base of the mountain, she parked and then began her climb. It was the perfect day—enough white clouds to give her a break from the sun's heat while still providing some beauty in the sky. The switchback path alternated between flat and up with patches of flowers dotting the way. A few springs of water provided her with some tranquil spots to have a clear drink.

When Danita reached her favorite spot in the field of flowers, she lay down, crossed her arms over her chest, and inhaled deeply. Danita could almost feel the stress leach out of her body as the floating clouds mesmerized her—that was until Angelique's comments came back to her. Maybe using bad for the sake of good wasn't healthy, but she didn't have a choice. Did she?

If she didn't find some relief from her increasing darkness, she might never locate Wendy, and a life with Griffin could never be.

DANITA'S PHONE RANG the next morning, jarring her out of a rather unpleasant dream. In this nightmare, Sanditra was attempting to make Danita stop time so that she could kill some animal. Of course, she'd refused to kill the rabbit, and that defiance on her part caused untold pain, but it was worth it not to have to take an innocent creature's life.

Shaking herself awake, she answered the phone. It was work. "Hey, Marie."

"You must be psychic," her boss said.

"Oh, yeah? Why's that?"

"Malpan Mining just called. Their receptionist is sick, and they need a replacement."

Instead of the excitement at achieving her goal, trepidation and guilt assaulted her. "I'm sorry for her but happy for me." Marie gave her the details. "I'll be there in a few. Thank you!"

Her boss chuckled. "Have fun with your miner friend."

For a second, Danita believed Marie had found out about Griffin, but then remembered Danita had mentioned her friend who worked in the mine there. "I plan to work, not have fun."

As soon as she disconnected, Danita rushed to get ready. When she arrived at the Malpan Mining office, the door was locked. While she could have used some of her magic to unlock it, she decided to only use her talents when absolutely necessary. She had to curb her desires whenever possible.

Gravel crunched on the drive, and she spun around. A truck was pulling in that had a Malpan Mining symbol on the door. A rather short man exited. While he was thick around the middle, he looked strong rather than fat.

He glanced at her. "Are you the replacement for Gianna?"

Danita guessed that was the name of his secretary. "Yes, sir."

"Good. Come in."

He flipped on the office light. "Do you know how to answer a phone?"

That was a bit insulting. "Malpan Mining, how may I help you?" she said in a high, lilting voice. She swore Malpan almost smiled.

"You'll do. Many of the clients waltz in unannounced. Have them sit in the outer office, and then knock on my door to tell me who's there."

"I can do that." This might be the easiest job yet—and possibly the most boring.

"Good."

For the first two hours, no one stopped in, which gave Danita time to study everything on Gianna's computer. Unfortunately, there was no mention of a second mine. No financials were listed either, implying an accountant was off site. Danita was unable to find out his or her name either. Crap. She wished she had, because most likely that person would be aware of this secret mine.

Close to five, a man with a straggly beard rushed in. If she had to guess from the dirty plaid shirt, he worked underground. "How can I help you?" she asked with as much cheer as possible.

"I'm here to see the boss."

Just as Danita pushed back her chair to announce him, he barreled past her and barged into Malpan's office. She rushed to the door to say she hadn't condoned this rude man's actions, but before she could, he slammed the door in her face. Okay, that didn't go well.

A few shouts sounded, causing her to remain by the door. If only she had the talent to walk through walls, she'd be home free.

"Two of them aren't doing as we've asked," said the mystery man.

"Why isn't Balkin there?" Malpan shot back.

Balkin? It sounded as if he'd been named after some star in the universe.

"Fuck if I know. I told him to put another spell on these men to keep them docile, but he's nowhere to be found."

Holy crap. Balkin could be Sanditra's replacement.

A hand slapped the table. "Then find him and drag his ass in there. I can't afford to have any rebellion, do you hear?" Hell, people in the parking lot could hear. "Then tell him I need him. He needs to do a renewal spell for me."

A renewal spell for Malpan? What was that about? From the

context, they were discussing the captive men and only the men. As much as Danita wanted one of them to mention where this secret mine was located, there would be no reason for them to do so.

She rushed back to her desk, sat down, and picked up the office phone pretending to be speaking with someone. The door to Mr. Malpan's office opened a minute later. Without giving it any thought, she closed her eyes, said her chant, and waved a hand. When she opened them up, the world had more or less come to a halt. The bearded newcomer was close to the main entrance. Not wanting to miss her chance, Danita rushed in front of him, snapped his photo, and then returned to her seat. She waved her hand once more, and the mine worker strode out, unaware of what had just happened.

Now all she had to do was find out this man's name and let Griffin do the rest.

Chapter Seven

THE NEXT DAY, Danita went back to Malpan Mines in the hopes the bearded man would return to update the boss on whether Balkin had succeeded in taming the slaves. She also hoped that her imagination hadn't gotten the best of her, and that this Balkin dude wasn't just some overseer in the regular mine. She snapped her fingers. Her friend, Carlton, who worked in the Malpan Mines would know.

After carefully composing her text, she sent him a message. Less than a minute later, she received a response: *Never heard of any Balkin. We should grab a drink and catch up.* Darn. Carlton might not be married, but after meeting Griffin, Danita had no interest in anyone else. Unsure of how to respond she just wrote: *I'll text you.*

By lunchtime, her nerves were strung tight. Every time the front door opened, she half expected Griffin to rush in and demand to know what she was doing there. At first, she was happy that he hadn't called or stopped by. All he had to do was look at her with those gorgeous brown eyes of his and she'd have told him the truth. When she revealed what she'd done, he'd really see what an evil person she was. What kind of white lighter would put a sick curse on an innocent girl in order to get a job? A bad one.

It was time to lift the curse and have Gianna return tomorrow. Danita found the packet of herbs she'd left in the receptionist's desk drawer. Concentrating, she mentally recited the words to reverse the spell. Not only wasn't it fair to the innocent woman, Danita didn't think she was going to learn the location of the mine even if she stayed a month. It certainly didn't seem as if Gianna knew of the secret location either.

Once her time was up, she said goodbye to Mr. Malpan and then returned home. Too bad her mood remained foul. Other than being convinced Malpan was guilty, she was no closer to locating the men. Not only that, her white light was leaving her faster than ever. Even if Wendy walked into her apartment in the next five minutes, Danita probably shouldn't be around her. No telling what might happen to a good person. Even dead, Danita's dark lighter torturer was affecting her.

While she should call Griffin to tell him what she'd learned in the hopes he could find the name of the man who'd stormed Malpan's office, she wasn't ready to hear how she never should have done what she'd done—and he'd be right.

After grabbing a bottle of wine from the cabinet, along with a glass, she settled down in front of the crappy television to watch a movie. It was going to be a long night, and she could only hope the nightmares stayed away.

"YOU HIKED UP to your mountain retreat area," Dr. Aminor said the next afternoon at their therapy session—therapy sessions Griffin had insisted on paying for. "How did that go?"

"Good. I could feel my white light keeping steady. I wish I could move up there permanently, but it's not practical. It's only accessible by foot." Danita sent out a rueful laugh. "Though being by myself might prevent me from thinking more dark thoughts."

Her therapist leaned forward. "Are you saying these bad urges are coming more often?"

Keeping everything to herself wasn't healthy. "Yes." It was time to come clean. "I did something the other day I'm not proud of."

"What was that?"

While Dr. Aminor kept her emotions fairly well hidden, Danita didn't miss the therapist's wince when Danita mentioned the spell she'd put on Gianna. "I only stayed two days."

"Am I to assume that using your darkness didn't help you at all then?"

"I actually did learn something important. I'm more convinced than ever that there is indeed a secret mine where men are being used as slaves." She told the good doctor her theory, but she didn't tell her the initial information came from Griffin.

"What do the authorities say?"

"A friend of mine is handling that end."

"I see. What is your next move?"

Danita blew out a breath. "I don't have a next move."

"Maybe it is for the best," Dr. Aminor said.

Maybe it was—for her, but not for the men being held captive.

When Danita left the office, she was more unsettled than ever. Some powerful need drew her to Griffin. Just because he hadn't called or stopped by the last two days, she saw no reason not to drop in on him. After all, turnabout was fair play. Besides, she wanted to see the inside of his big mining operation. She yearned to learn another side to him. In addition to being the protector, she bet Griffin could be ruthless yet fair in the business world.

He'd told her he was working out of the remote site instead of at the main office downtown. Thankfully, it took her less time than expected to reach the mine. Danita parked in front of the office, but she had no idea if Griffin would even be there this time of day. He'd mentioned that he often visited potential clients, taking them out to lunch or sharing a few drinks.

When she stepped inside the building, she told the receptionist that she'd like to see Griffin.

"He's right down the hall."

As she headed down the short hallway, a door opened, and his sister Nessa stepped out. "Hey, Danita. What are you doing here?"

At least she sounded friendly. "I'm looking for Griffin."

Nessa smiled. "I'll walk you there."

Danita followed Nessa to the end of the hallway where a double door with Griffin's nameplate was prominently displayed off to the side. Nessa knocked. When someone mumbled something inside, she pushed it open and then peeked her head in. "Someone is here to see you," his sister said in an overly cheerful tone. Nessa faced her. "Go on in."

It was stupid to be nervous, but what she was about to tell Griffin would make him mad, and Danita wasn't sure she could handle more drama today.

Griffin pushed back his chair and came around his desk. "Is something wrong?"

Why did he always assume the worst? "No, I just haven't seen you in a few days."

The tension around his eyes and mouth softened. "You came to socialize?"

That implied she'd been too self-centered to ever enjoy herself. "Kind of. Okay, not entirely."

His joy evaporated. Damn. "Sit down and tell me." He leaned a hip on his desk and peered down at her.

"Before you yell, hear me out," she said.

"Oh, shit. What did you do? Don't tell me you stalked Gregory Malpan."

Yup. This wasn't going to be pleasant. She inhaled deeply and then blew out a breath. "Kind of. I snagged a temporary job at his mining company for two days." She held up a hand. "Don't worry. He suspected nothing. I learned something however, which is why I'm here."

His lips thinned. "Go on."

She explained about the bearded man and how he had just barged in. "I couldn't hear the whole conversation, but this man said that two of the men weren't doing what they were told. But here's the interesting part. Malpan told this bearded man that he needed to have Balkin put another spell on the men."

From the way Griffin's eyes lost focus for a second, he was trying to put all of the pieces together. "He used the word *spell?*"

"Yes. A white lighter can't miss that word."

"True."

"The problem was that this Balkin dude hadn't shown up in a while, and Malpan demanded this bearded guy find him."

"Interesting. Do you think this is happening at this secret mine?"

"Very possibly. I contacted a friend of mine who works in the regular copper mine, and he'd never heard of anyone by the name of Balkin."

"I see. Any mention of where this secret mine is located?"

"No." She fished out her phone. "But I have a photo of him. I thought maybe you could have your cop cousin run facial rec or something."

What looked like admiration crossed his face. "I will." Griffin tapped a few keys to transfer the photo to his computer. "I'll send this to Logan. He can do his magic on this."

"I hope it helps."

"Me too." Griffin leaned back on his hands. "Why aren't you at work now?"

"I only made the secretary sick for two days, because I felt bad she had to suffer even that long."

Griffin stilled. "You made her sick so you could replace her?" His voice rose with each word.

Shit. She hadn't meant for that to slip out but keeping secrets from the man who believed they were mates wouldn't be smart. "Kind of. It was just a little spell. I know, I know. That was wrong of me, but this darkness inside me is growing stronger by the day. I couldn't help it." Or else she didn't really want to stop it. "Soon, even you'll need to stay away from me or chance being tainted." Her chin trembled at that thought, though in truth she didn't know if her darkness could spread to someone else.

Griffin slipped off the edge of his desk. "That isn't going to happen. We'll fight this together. There has to be a way to rid your body of this evil. Sanditra is dead. How long can a spell last anyway?"

"I have no idea. Even though she is dead, I think all she did was inject me with her poisonous thoughts. From there, they grew. It's kind of like a dark cancer."

He cupped her shoulders, drew her to a stand, and hugged her. "Don't worry."

Easy for him to say, though she was thankful that he seemed to have forgiven her. "Thank you."

He leaned back. "I have just the thing," he said with surprising cheer.

"What?" Her tone came out sounding sullen, and she never liked a whiner.

"How about we get out of here for a few hours to clear our heads?"

She wasn't sure why he'd want to do that. It sounded so whimsical, and Griffin Caspian was anything but. "Are you planning on looking for this secret mine?"

"No. At least not with you in tow."

"You know I can handle myself." She puffed out her chest and lifted her hand to stop time, but Griffin clasped her hand and brought her palm to his lips.

"I know you can slow time, but if trouble was near, all that would do is help to allow you time to hide. And that's assuming someone doesn't attack you from behind, like that wolf Changeling did."

Why did he always have to come up with such logical reasons for her to stay out of trouble? "Fine. Where were you planning on us going, if not to look for this mine?"

A small smile lifted his lips, and her heart melted. "I believe you mentioned a meadow in the mountains that you like to go to and think."

When had she told him that? It didn't matter. "There is."

Griffin released her hand and stepped over to his desk where he picked up a box that was wrapped in purple and pink paper. A small white sprig of dried flowers adorned the top. It was beautiful.

He handed it to her. "I saw this and couldn't resist buying it for you. I had planned to give it to you later, but I think now would be the perfect time."

"A present for me? What is it?"

He let out a short laugh. "You have to open it to find out."

Danita's fingers trembled. She couldn't remember the last time anyone had given her anything. While her dad was still alive, they weren't on speaking terms anymore. As for her mom, she left right after Danita was born. Presents were not something she was used to getting in her home—even on her birthday. She tore off the paper and was stunned by the beauty of the clay figurine. It was a woman sitting among the flowers.

She looked up at Griffin. "This is amazing. It looks just like my favorite spot."

Griffin grinned. "I was at the Four Sisters Pottery Shop, and as soon as I saw it, I thought of you."

"Thank you."

Without thinking about her dark light or the issues she was facing, she threw her arms around his neck. He embraced her and held her close. His powerful chest and heated body electrified her. While the thought of kissing him entered her mind, she wasn't quite there yet.

Griffin must have sensed her reticence because he let go. "Tell me where this special place is."

"It's off Canyon Cove Road. From there it's about a thirty-minute hike to this field that is about halfway up the mountain."

He glanced down at her clothes. "I don't think those shoes will give you enough traction for a hike. How about we fly?" He held up a hand. "In case you're wondering, I've never dropped anything or anyone in my life. You can keep your eyes closed the whole time if you want."

If she did that, it would make it difficult for her to give him directions. Danita hadn't always been so timid. It was only after Sanditra changed her that she'd become paranoid and afraid. She inhaled deeply. If she were in Dr. Aminor's office right now, her therapist would tell her to go for it. "How long will it take if we fly?"

"Six or seven minutes, tops."

She could do that. "Then let's do it."

Griffin smiled and then looked at her with such warmth in those brown and teal eyes of his that she almost threw caution to the wind and kissed him.

"Maybe you should leave the gift in your car. I don't want you to drop it."

"That would be bad."

With his hand on her back, Griffin led her outside. While she was tempted to tell him she'd stop home and change, she needed to do this. Being pressed up against his body for that long might wake up some long-lost urges though, and she wasn't sure if that would be a good thing or not.

Chapter Eight

GRIFFIN COULDN'T BELIEVE his good luck. Danita had turned him down so many times, claiming flying just wasn't her thing. He could respect that, but he had figured that the stress from being held captive first, and then her cousin disappearing, added to the rabid Changeling wolf attack, had made her skittish in general. To keep her anxiety from flaring, he would fly fairly low and not do any maneuvers.

Once she placed her present in the car, she faced him. "I'm ready."

"I'm going to shift, so don't freak."

Danita tilted her head, as if to say, *really?* "I've lived in Tarradon my whole life. It's not like I haven't seen dragons flying overhead all the time."

"I know, but I'll be close. Never mind. Once I shift, I'll reach out with my claw and pick you up. You don't have to hold on, but I'll bet you'll want to."

Danita lifted her chin to show him that she could be brave. "Since I might have to help you locate my favorite spot, I guess I should face downward."

He hadn't expected that. "Okay, but if you want me to turn you around, carry you against my chest, or point to where I need to go just tap my talon three times."

A brief smile crossed her lips. "Got it."

Griffin stepped back and shifted, hoping she didn't turn tail and jump in her car. To Danita's credit she remained in place. He approached her and held out his claw. When she opened her arms, his heart swelled. She might be able to embrace the dragon life after all. He wouldn't put a time frame however on her acceptance of them being mates.

With much care, he picked her up. When Danita didn't yell or squirm, he flapped his wings and took off, trying not to accelerate too fast. Once they were a few hundred feet above the ground, he leveled off and headed toward her favorite field. He knew relatively where her place was located. As he'd estimated, he was flying above the mountainous area seven minutes later.

Danita pointed to a spot. "That's it," she shouted.

Pleased she sounded excited, he spotted the colorful flowers and landed. After he released her, Griffin stepped back and shifted. When she didn't say anything, he feared she might be in shock.

"Are you okay?"

Danita held out her arms, lifted her face to the sun, and spun around once. "That was incredible."

"Really?"

"Yes, really. What's not to love? I can't believe I've been afraid all this time."

"I couldn't be more pleased." As much as he wanted her to tell him about every sensation she experienced, he didn't want her to think he needed his ego stroked. "Show me where you like to sit."

"Right here." Danita plopped down onto her back.

Griffin joined her and studied the sky, pretending to look at it through her eyes. "The sky is really blue, isn't it?"

"It's the same color as when you flew through it," she shot back, sounding almost flirty.

"Good point." This mountain top retreat seemed to affect her on a cellular level, and he certainly didn't want to break the tentative connection they were having.

When Griffin rested his head on his folded arms, only then did he pay attention to all of the red, pink, purple, white, and yellow flowers that seemed to almost wrap themselves around the two of them. Their fragrance helped relax him too, despite his dragon going crazy being inches from his mate—both on their backs no less.

Kiss her, his dragon urged.

I want to, but it's too soon.

You've kissed her before.

You have a point, but I want both of us to enjoy the view, the smells, and the fresh air before I make my move.

I can wait, his dragon said, *but not for long.*

Griffin had never known his animal to be this pushy. It made sense though, since he was finally with their mate. The clouds scudded overhead. "Do you see any images in the clouds?" he asked.

"Mmm. Those parallel clouds look like bars," she said, pointing to ones toward the east.

That was depressing. "Maybe you should attempt to see more pleasant things—like a funny face, a flower, or a cute animal."

She laughed a little, and it lightened his mood. "You sound like my therapist."

"Smart woman. Speaking of which. How is that going?"

Danita rolled onto her side and propped her head up with her hand. "Better, actually. I can't tell you how much I appreciate you insisting that I do therapy. Needless to say, I couldn't have gone without your financial help and emotional support."

While she'd thanked him many times before, this time Danita sounded the sincerest, almost as if she was finally emerging from a fog herself. As much as Griffin wanted to pull her on top of him and kiss her, he wanted to give her time to enjoy this special place.

Normally, Griffin didn't give into such fantasy, but Danita brought out his light heartedness. Even he understood that he needed to let go sometimes. Being the eldest in the family brought with it a lot of responsibility. Today however, was going to be about whimsy—assuming he was capable of doing that.

Griffin studied the sky. The image of the fallen sales whipped across his mind, but he refused to dwell on it for now. This was time he wanted to spend with Danita.

Then he saw it. He pointed to a cloud configuration in the air.

"See that one there? It looks like a breed of dog I've heard about that they have on Earth. It's called a poodle."

She studied it for a moment. "I can see the head, body, and tail. You have a good imagination."

"Not usually. You bring it out in me," Griffin said as he rolled toward her, their lips less than a foot apart. While it seemed as if they were close, the distance was immense.

"That is sweet," she said, sounding relaxed for the first time.

He inhaled, letting the smells soothe and calm his dragon. As if his animal was controlling his thoughts, he dragged a knuckle down her cheek. "You are so beautiful."

She looked away. "You don't have to say things like that."

"What are you talking about? I could get lost in those hazel eyes, which by the way, are almost green."

"It's the reflection of the green flower stems."

Griffin lowered his hand to her shoulder and pulled her closer, waiting for her to stop him. "Don't do that, Danita. I see you as this pretty imp with a spray of freckles across her nose. I know you are always fussing with your hair and don't like the way it curls, but I love it. You are untamed, wild, smart, and good for me. I'm the one who is too serious. I've been told too many times that I always have a scowl on my face."

She sort of chuckled. "That's kind of true, but I like the way—"

He pressed a finger to her lips. "Let me finish. I know I'm overly protective and probably too concerned about the Caspian mines, but ever since you walked into my life, I've shifted my focus. I've even dared to dream about what it could be like if we were together."

He needed to shut up. Her face was already turning several shades of red. The only way to convince her that he was falling in love with her was to show her. Griffin lowered his hand to her waist and pulled, moving them together.

When Danita didn't resist, he kissed her.

DANITA SHOULD HAVE stopped Griffin, but she didn't. Why? Because she wanted to kiss him again, though she had no idea what had happened to make her be this bold. Maybe it was having performed a spell to harm someone—even if it was for a good cause—that made her realize she needed to head down a different path. She knew what she had done was wrong. Her therapist knew it. And Griffin knew it. It was time to change—assuming she could.

The air blew across their faces, carrying with it the sweet combination of fresh air, flowers, and grass. Danita raised her hand and placed it on Griffin's shoulder. When she pressed her fingers into his muscular arm, waves of lust filled her. It might be the location, or maybe having flown in the grasp of a dragon shifter, but she could almost feel light building inside her—and she wanted more. Much more.

Danita wasn't aware of moving her leg, but somehow it found its way on top of his thigh. Griffin grunted. His eyes turned into swirls of teal as their lips fully engaged. When he begged for entrance, Danita threw caution to the wind and opened her mouth. The first touch of his tongue swamped her with emotions she'd long forgotten—ones of longing, caring, and a bit of love. Griffin was so amazing, but even she knew they couldn't be together until she banished the darkness, and that would start when she found Wendy.

With his breaths coming out hard and fast, Griffin broke the kiss. His eyes flashed teal with streaks of gold and rust running through them. "If I don't stop kissing you now, I might not be able to."

Her pulse pounded at the whole idea that he wanted her so much. It overwhelmed her and scared her at the same time. "I understand."

The idea of making love with him wasn't in the cards right now for her either. Unfortunately, the kiss had woken up parts of her body that she'd thought she'd long forgotten. No doubt Griffin Caspian was one dangerous man where she was concerned.

Danita couldn't let him think he hadn't affected her though.

"That was nice," she said.

The corner of his lip lifted, and his eyes sparkled. "That so?"

Her paranoia came out of nowhere and made her lean away from him and then sit up. "Yes, but you were right to stop. I think we should probably go."

"Are you sure?" he kept his tone non-threatening.

"Yes."

Griffin stood and helped her up. Too bad his touch reminded her of what she might never have.

"Ready?" he asked.

Not really, but now she was the one who feared she might say or do something she'd later regret if she stayed here with him. "Yes."

He stepped back and shifted. This time she walked up to him, grabbed his claw, and allowed him to lift her in his grasp. The security of his chest made her want to stay in his arms—or rather his claws—for a long time.

The trip back wasn't nearly as scary as before. In fact, Danita enjoyed being in his grasp, remembering that memorable kiss.

Her feet touched the ground without her being aware they'd arrived back to the Caspian mines. How did that happen? It wasn't as if Griffin had put a memory blocking spell on her.

He shifted and faced her. "I want you to know that I am doing everything I can to find Wendy. I asked my brother Logan to look into her phone records."

"Why? I'd assumed the cops had already checked them out and had found nothing."

He smiled. "Logan is better. Why don't you come in for a minute and I'll tell you what he found out? I could fix us something to drink. I know I'm parched from all that flying."

She didn't buy it, but spending more time with him when others were around was safe. Right now, Danita didn't trust herself. "Sure."

In companionable silence, they entered the main building. Instead of heading toward his office, they went to another room that was a well-equipped break room. "What would you like to drink?" he asked.

She didn't want him to go to too much trouble. Danita drank

coffee as well as tea. "Whatever you're having."

"Water?"

She hadn't thought of that, but it worked. "With ice, please."

Once he fixed their drinks, he motioned for her to sit on the settee next to him where his large frame took up most of the space on the seat. Danita needed to block the pulses charging through her and focus on her cousin's dilemma. "Tell me what Logan learned."

"Just that her last two calls were to a Chad Lansing."

"Chad? Interesting."

"You know him?"

"Not personally," she said, "but he and Wendy were good friends. They dated a couple of times, but it wasn't anything serious. Both went into the relationship knowing that if their mate came along, they'd break up."

"I didn't know Wendy was a shifter."

"She's a wolf shifter." Danita sipped the water, and only then realized how thirsty she was. After she downed half of it, she set it on the coffee table.

"What else do you know about Chad?"

"He works at the fire department in Search and Rescue."

Griffin leaned back, his gaze moving around the room. "You said Wendy is a journalist, right?"

"Yes."

"What story was she working on? It might have been what caused her capture."

Danita blew out a breath. "I don't know. I asked Wendy, but she said one of her sources told her something that she didn't want to— or rather couldn't—discuss. I had to respect that."

"Sure." Griffin lifted his water and chugged it down. "What do you say we try to find this Chad person? He might be involved in what she was working on. Hell, he could be her source."

"I doubt it, but who am I to say? Wendy had her secrets." She stood. "Let's go."

Chapter Nine

G RIFFIN WASN'T ALL that optimistic that a former boyfriend-turned-friend would be a journalist's confidante, but if it meant Griffin could spend more time with Danita by checking him out, he was good with it. Danita insisted on driving, because she wanted to have her car in town. That worked for him. Griffin had no problem flying back.

"I forgot to ask," she said as she pulled into a parking space a block from the fire station.

"About?"

"That photo I gave you of the man who told Malpan about Balkin. Did you ever find out who he was?"

"Not yet. I gave it to Logan to run facial recognition, but he came up with nothing. Sorry. Logan promised to continue searching though."

"Thank you."

She cut the engine and slipped out. Griffin said nothing about requesting to always let him open the door for her, since he wanted to protect her. He attributed the hasty exit to her excitement at the potential lead.

On foot, they headed toward the fire station. As much as he wanted to take her hand, he didn't. The sparse amount of conversation on the way to town implied she was still processing the kiss—or was she thinking about what Logan had found out? Griffin decided to go with the kiss. Hell, his scales were still throwing off random bursts of rust. Thankfully that color was close to his natural skin tone, so maybe neither Danita nor anyone else would notice. It would be highly embarrassing to have his scales flash, as well as his eye color turning teal, not to mention his talons almost poking out of the ends of his fingertips. He tried chastising his dragon for acting so sexual, but the animal wouldn't listen. That kiss had incited him something fierce.

A few minutes later, they entered the station. Two men were washing the fire truck, and Griffin walked up to one of them—one who happened to be a dragon shifter. "I'm looking for a Chad Lansing."

The tall, beefy man in the blue uniformed shirt smiled and held out his hand. "That's me. What can I do for you?"

Griffin motioned for Danita to join them. "I'm Griffin Caspian and this is Danita Warren."

His eyes widened slightly. "Wendy Oprander's cousin?"

"Yes."

Chad opened his mouth, inhaled, and then closed it. Griffin wouldn't be surprised if he was about to ask how she was doing after her incarceration a few months back, but he probably realized now wasn't the time or place to bring up that bad memory. "How can I help you?"

"Were you aware that Wendy has gone missing?"

His face lost color. "No! When? I'm in Search and Rescue and never received a call. Can I do anything now?"

Griffin liked this young man. "I doubt she is lost in the woods. We have reason to believe foul play might have been involved. We did look through her phone records and found that she called you recently. Twice in fact. Can you tell us what it was about? Unless it was personal."

Chad stabbed a hand through his hair. "She called to see if I had dealt with any unresolved missing men cases in the last five months."

Danita stiffened beside him, and every fiber of Griffin's Guardian being shot to life. "What did you say?"

He blew out a breath. "I told her I would speak with my boss to see what information I could release."

"I'd love to know what that was. It could be important in finding her."

He glanced around and then nodded. "Please don't share this, but in the last five months, there have been five reported cases of men who've gone missing. We looked for days, but came up empty-handed. The police have no clues either."

Only five men? "Can you give me their names?"

His brows rose. "Are you planning on looking for them?"

"Yes."

"Excuse me for a minute then. I'll get the list for you."

Once Chad left, Griffin turned to Danita who was worrying her fingers and looking off to the side. "What are you thinking?" he asked.

"I find it hard to believe that the men reported missing are the ones who were taken by Malpan."

"Why is that?"

"When one of my family members went missing, I immediately went to the police. You'd think there would be thirty requests instead of five."

He'd thought the same thing. "I'll follow up with Anderson to see how many were reported. It's possible the men were loners without any family in town. I'll call the other Provinces too to see if their relatives contacted the authorities."

"Smart."

Chad returned and handed Griffin a piece of paper. "Here is the list of men who are still missing."

Griffin scanned the paper but didn't recognize any of the names. He folded it up and stuffed it in his pants pocket. "Thanks. Do you know if any of the men are shifters?"

"Yes, in fact all five are. It's why we kept looking. We figured if they were stuck in the woods, they could shift and survive. The date of their disappearance is listed also."

Griffin held out his hand. "I appreciate this."

"I hope you figure out what happened to them. Let us know if you do." Chad shook his hand and then Danita's. "I'm worried about your cousin. I feel as if I should go out and look in case there wasn't foul play."

"That is so sweet of you, but I'm pretty sure she was abducted."

"That's terrible."

Griffin nodded. "If we need your help, you'll be the first we call."

"Thanks."

Griffin and Danita left the station, and the bright light almost hurt his eyes. "Do you want to see if Logan can unearth any information about these men?" he asked.

"Sure, but how do you think this relates to Wendy's disappearance exactly? There were only five men missing instead of thirty."

"I can't be sure, but if she was snooping around, she might have gotten too close."

"To Malpan?"

He didn't want her to go there. No telling what Danita would do. "I don't know if it was Malpan, but too close to whoever was involved in the disappearance of these men."

"The cops spoke with Wendy's boss about what she was working on, but he said it had nothing to do with missing men."

"Interesting. Come on. Want to fly back?"

She hesitated and then smiled. "Sure." She looked around. "You're going to shift on the sidewalk?"

"No. We'll drive back to SinCas and take off from there. It's a lot quicker."

"And it will use less gas."

Danita's more upbeat personality was shining through and that made him happy. The trip to the mountains seemed to have done wonders for her mental health.

When they reached the SinCas building, he suggested she park underground. His motivation for suggesting it had been to impress her about the perks of being with him. Not heroic at all, but his thought processes were off lately when he was around Danita.

They took the elevator to the top floor and then climbed the last flight of stairs to the rooftop. "I think it would have been faster to drive," she said, a little out of breath.

Damn. He hadn't thought about the inconvenience of it all. He just wanted to hold her in his claws even it was only for a few minutes. "You might be right." He added a chuckle to keep it upbeat.

On the roof he shifted, swooped her up, and took off. He liked how her body no longer tensed when she was in the air with him. All too soon they landed. When he set her down, stepped back and shifted, Danita smiled. Griffin tried to memorize the shine in her eyes and vowed to put that look on her face every day for the rest of her life.

"I'm really getting into this flying stuff."

He never would have guessed. "I'm so glad. Let's see if Logan is in."

Inside the Caspian mining office, Griffin knocked on Logan's door and then pushed it open. His brother looked up. The moment he noticed Danita, a smug as hell smile filled his face. Logan had suggested many times Griffin and Danita actually go out on a date. Now they had. Knowing his brother, Logan would think it was all his doing.

"This is a surprise, but from your face, bro, it's not a social call."

Griffin pulled the piece of paper from his pocket. "Not really. Long story short, we have a list of five men who went missing within the last five months and were never found. All were shifters." He told him his theory about how Wendy might have been investigating these men's disappearance, which was possibly why she'd been taken. She knew too much.

Logan's brows pinched. "Are you thinking these men might also have a connection to *our* problem?"

Griffin appreciated that his brother was trying to be discreet about the idea that the reason their copper sales had fallen was because Malpan's mine was using slaves to help lower his cost, but

Logan's discretion wasn't needed. Griffin believed in keeping Danita in the loop. "Yes. It's possible these are five of the thirty or so men who were captured by who we suspect was Malpan."

Logan reached for the paper and then studied it. "What would you like to know? Seems to me you have their names, dates when they went missing, and everything."

"We want to see if the kidnapper is only taking able-bodied men who have little to no family in town, or did these five men legitimately wander into the woods, never to be seen again? If I were trying to find some slaves, I'd pick men without a lot of family ties in town. It's possible these men were unemployed. That way, fewer people would notice what happened to them. The fact that they are shifters helps prove our hypothesis."

Logan nodded. "Sounds good. Why don't you two sit in the break room while I do my thing? Or better yet, show Danita around the property. It might take me some time to check them all out."

"Sure." Griffin couldn't ask Danita to stand there and wait. As they left Logan to do his thing, Griffin checked his watch. "It's a little early for dinner, but we haven't eaten all day. Are you up for a little food?"

"Absolutely."

"What's your preference? I'm buying since you were so kind to indulge in my search today."

"Are you kidding? I want to be involved in finding my cousin."

If her being involved meant hanging out with him, then great. If she planned to do anything again like stalk Gregory Malpan, then no. "Pick a place."

"The Hillside Café in town?"

"Let's do it." It wasn't a place he would have chosen, but the food there was good. At this hour, they might even be able to chat without people overhearing them.

After returning to the SinCas building, he shifted, and together they headed over to the café. Being with Danita was amazing. Griffin had never realized how much he had been missing in his life by not having found his mate. But it wasn't until very recently that Danita seemed to have come out of her angry and depressed mood over what Sanditra had done to her. It was as if the attack by the Changeling werewolf woke her up somehow. She seemed to have decided not to be a victim anymore and instead embrace life. Griffin couldn't be more pleased.

Thankfully, the café wasn't too busy. The place was always jammed for lunch, but not so much for dinner, which fit into his plans nicely. He led her over to a table in the corner and sat in the chair facing the entrance. Even though he could sense when any shifter entered, he feared being near Danita might distract him.

After the waitress took their drink orders, Danita threaded her fingers together. "Even if you learn that these five men were healthy with no family to speak of, how are you going to go about finding them?" she asked.

He leaned back in his chair. "That is the million Denlar question. If we believe these men are in some underground mine being held captive, we need to find this mine."

"Have you looked yet?"

"To be honest, I didn't know it existed until recently, so no. I do plan to do a few fly overs, but unless I see some mining equipment or sheds in an otherwise vacant area, I'm not sure how I can locate it."

"Too bad I don't know any white lighter who can sense minerals in the ground."

He snapped his fingers. "Nessa actually can. In fact, her senses alerted her to gold under the ground on our property."

Danita's eyes sparkled. "Why not ask her to help?"

His excitement from a moment ago evaporated. He shook his head. "Unfortunately, Nessa needs to be on the ground to detect it, and we have no idea what province the mine is in. If the other twenty-five men came from all over Tarradon, our job will be next to impossible."

Danita slumped in her seat. "Damn." She jerked upright. "How about if you follow Malpan? You said you can fly undetected, right? I would think he'd go to the mine at some point to check on things."

"You have a good point, and while it's true I can cloak myself, it takes a tremendous amount of energy to remain hidden. That's not to say I won't try. I'd like something a little quicker if possible. The guilty party—who we can't be positive is Malpan—might only visit the mine once a month, if at all. No, there has to be some way to narrow down its location faster than that."

Their server brought over their drinks and then took their order. They both sat in silence, clearly trying to figure out the best tactic. Griffin appreciated how willing Danita was to work through the options with him. It helped having someone to bounce ideas off of.

Griffin's cell rang, and he picked it up. "It's Logan." He pressed the receive call button. "What did you find out?"

"Hey, you don't even sound impressed at how fast I worked."

Logan was a genius and probably didn't get the recognition he deserved. "I'm sorry. Wow, that was fast! What did you find?"

His brother chuckled. "What you guessed was right. If I go by their photos, they all look to be relatively young—young enough to be good workers in a mine. The people who called to report these men missing were neighbors, not relatives."

"Interesting. It seems as if they were handpicked—assuming these are the men who were abducted and enslaved. I'd like to take the photos to Arthur Gonzalez and see if he recognizes them as the men he and the others captured and then sold to Malpan."

It didn't matter that Gonzalez claimed these men were in their shifter form. Griffin hoped Gonzalez would slip up and identify the men.

Danita's eyes lit up the moment he mentioned Malpan's name.

"I'll send them to your phone."

"Great work, Logan."

"Do you want me to look into the other provinces for the other missing persons?"

"Hold off for a bit. If Gonzalez admits to kidnapping these five men, then our next step will be to find the mine. The other missing men might be there. We have no idea if the captor is still using them or if he sold them."

"Horrible thought. Let me know."

"Will do." Griffin disconnected and looked up at Danita's eager face. "You heard?"

"Yes. When are we going to interview this Gonzalez man?"

Oh, no. "There is no *we* here. Hell, Gonzalez wouldn't even talk to the cops. Only me or Declan."

Since Griffin wanted to spend time with her, he thought it best if he tossed the job of speaking with Gonzalez to Declan. Tomorrow would be soon enough though. Right now, Griffin had other plans— plans that involved his mate.

Chapter Ten

DANITA COULDN'T RECALL the last time she'd seen Griffin so excited. Not only did he really love to help others, he also worked hard to make sure he contributed to the success of Caspian Mining. Could this man be any more perfect? Only if he let her help more.

"Are *you* going to the jail now to speak with Gonzalez?"

"No. This is our time together. I'll call Declan later to see if he can stop by tomorrow. Even if I spoke with Gonzalez right now, and he said these were men he'd taken, there's not much I can do about it. I'd need help and a plan. That will require gathering my siblings and cousins to learn their thoughts."

"That would be awesome."

Their meal arrived and they both dug in. Danita hadn't realized how incredibly hungry she was. "This is good."

"It is. Thanks for suggesting we come here."

It was nice to have a normal conversation with Griffin where he wasn't telling her not to interfere in what should be police business. This time it seemed as if he'd decided to have the Guardians participate instead of going to the cops. Though once Declan spoke with Gonzalez, the cops might learn what was up.

Danita wolfed down her food, her mind spinning about what she could do to help and still be safe. Uh-oh. She looked up at Griffin. "You don't think anyone knows we've been asking around about these missing men do you?"

Griffin stilled. "Not unless someone at the fire department is in cahoots with the kidnapper."

She shivered. "There are a lot of loose ends. I mean, Logan was doing a search. His digging might have triggered some kind of computer alarm."

Griffin reached out and clasped her hand. "Danita, don't do this. You'll only work yourself up into a frenzy with what-if scenarios. Are you afraid someone will come after you like they might have with Wendy?"

"It's possible. I don't exactly have a great history with avoiding that kind of stuff."

Griffin pressed his lips together. "At least until this mess is solved, would you like me to stay with you? I'd be at work during the day—but you can come with me if you want, though it won't be exciting most of the time. At night, I'll spend it with you."

Holy hell! If he'd been anyone other than the man she deeply cared for, she would have jumped at the chance to have protection. If she agreed though, would he expect them to be intimate? Maybe the better question was whether she wanted to be intimate with him?

Since her body was vibrating from his touch, the answer was clear. It was time. "I'd like that."

The grin that spread across his face totally transformed his already handsome looks. She swore white light was pouring into her just from being with him. "Great. Let's finish eating, and then I'll pick up a few things I might need from my condo."

"Are you sure it won't be too inconvenient?" she asked.

He leaned forward. "Danita. We belong together."

"I know, but my place is pretty crappy."

"Is that the real reason you hesitated? You have to know by now that I would never do anything you don't want me to. I promise I'll be as good as I'm capable of being."

She smiled. "You're always good, Griffin Caspian."

His right eyebrow rose. "I didn't exactly behave myself on the mountain, now did I?"

"No, but I liked it. A lot."

As if the conversation embarrassed him, Griffin chowed down

the rest of his meal, focusing hard on the food. Danita wasn't able to finish her chicken since she was too excited about tonight. She'd been so focused on her issues of being dark that she hadn't realized how lonely she'd become. After tonight, that could all change.

GRIFFIN HOPED HE wasn't making a mistake in suggesting he stay with Danita, but the way her voice wavered, she sounded afraid. He would offer to sleep on the sofa. No way could he sleep next to her all night and get any rest. If he did, he'd have to hold her, kiss her, and then make love with her. If she wasn't ready, it could delay things from ever developing. If she was ready, his life just might change forever.

"Here we are," Griffin said as he opened the door to his condo. "It's a little sparse."

He didn't know why he wanted to apologize, but he'd never taken the time to decorate. Griffin always knew that the woman he ended up with would want to do the honors. One thing he was certain of was that Danita would love the large open concept along with the light pouring in the window during the day. However, no discerning woman would like his choice of minimalist furniture. Neither of his sisters liked it at all.

When Griffin flicked on the light, Danita drew in a large breath. "It's amazing."

Pride slammed into him. "It's not really decorated."

Damn. He should have just thanked her. Then it occurred to him that she might feel safer at his place. It required an eye scanner to get into the condo, a doorman to keep anyone out, and it had two bedrooms, allowing him to sleep in one and Danita in the other.

"Are you kidding me? You actually have a sofa with no rips in it. And that television is three times the size of the one I have."

Griffin moved closer and tried to keep his excitement controlled. "We could stay here if you like."

"Really? Are you sure?"

He chuckled. "Yes, I'm sure."

"That would be great, but that means I'd have to pick up a few things from my apartment."

"Let's go then." If he stayed at his place much longer, no telling what his dragon would insist they do. Hell, it would take all of his control just to walk out the door with her.

Because Danita's apartment was a half-mile away, they chose to walk. Once at her door, her hands shook as she tried to get the key into the lock.

"Let me do that for you." He unlocked her door, hoping he wasn't moving too fast when he suggested they stay together.

Without asking if he wanted a drink or suggest he take a seat, she dashed into the bedroom. That was okay. He didn't need any hospitality. He was sure she had a lot on her mind.

With Danita packing, he'd have time to tighten the screws on her door—a door that seemed none too sturdy. Griffin hoped that even after her cousin was found, and possibly the missing men, that she'd want to stay with him. Forever. Mating would take time, but the change in her in the last week had been profound.

After he found her small tool kit under the sink, he went to work on the door, trying to ignore her grunts of frustration. Too bad her sounds made him think of making love with her.

Enough was enough. Once he finished fixing the door, Griffin couldn't help but knock on her bedroom door. When she didn't answer, he pushed it open.

On the bed was her suitcase, stacked full of clothes. He smiled. "You know, you can always come back for more. If that doesn't work, I do have a washing machine."

"Sorry. I didn't mean to take so much time, but I couldn't decide what I needed."

Her frustration cut a hole in his heart. He strode up to her and pulled her into an embrace. "You don't have to apologize to me. Ever." When her body trembled, he kissed the top of her head.

"Having you hold me feels good," Danita said as she wrapped her arms around his back and buried her face against his chest.

Her embrace caused waves of longing and a bit of helplessness. He wanted so badly for this incredible woman to realize her potential. Hopefully, he could do something about that.

When he looked down at Danita, she lifted her head and parted her lips. His body heated and his scales flashed.

"Kiss me," he said, unable to control his need much longer.

Danita slid her hands from around his body up to his face and pulled him down to her level. Without a word, their lips met, and lust nearly felled him. The last time they'd kissed, he'd been the one to pull away. This time, he wanted her to be the one to stop, because he couldn't bring himself to ever let her go. Griffin wanted his mate more than anything.

Danita must not have been thinking straight either, because she pressed her body hard against his and opened her mouth, begging for entrance. If their tongues touched this time, he'd be lost. Instead of letting her decide as he'd hoped, Griffin leaned back an inch and whispered. "If I start, I know I won't be able to stop this time."

"I was hoping you'd say that."

Joy filled him. As much as he wanted to slam her against the door and drive into her, he wouldn't. Danita was fragile and deserved to be worshiped. "In that case, let's move the suitcase off the bed."

She stepped aside, and he cleared the bed in seconds. When he spun around to continue where they left off, she had her shoes off and her blouse half undone. Whoa.

Griffin had no idea what to make of it, but he wasn't going to tell her how to make love. He sat on the bed, ready to enjoy the most sensual experience of his life.

FOR THE FIRST time in a long time, Danita wanted to do what pleased her instead of doing what someone told her to do. Right now, that meant she wanted to be loved by Griffin. Over the past five months, he'd been patient—oh so patient—and caring and wonderful. She'd been too afraid that her issues might rub off on him, so she'd kept him at arm's length. Because he didn't seem to be affected adversely by being with her, she wasn't a threat to him!

When Griffin sat on the bed to watch, a rush of sexuality suffused her body. She'd never done a strip tease before, but she knew in her heart he'd never judge her. Because of all she'd been through, she'd lost a lot of weight and was very self-conscious about her small breasts and lack of curves, but from the way Griffin was smiling and how his scales were flashing, he didn't seem to notice.

Keeping her gaze on his face, she finished unbuttoning her blouse. Trying to be sexy, she slipped the material off her shoulders as slowly as possible and let the shirt fall. If she hadn't sucked at this, Danita might have moaned.

When his gaze dropped to her breasts, she covered them. It didn't matter she had on a padded bra, showing no more than a bathing suit top.

"You are so beautiful," Griffin whispered.

His teal eyes told her that he was telling the truth. Before she showed him everything, she stepped out of her pants. Now in plain white cotton panties and a pink bra, she wasn't sure if she should remove them or let him do the honors. Since Griffin's mouth had turned slack and one of his talons had poked out of his fingertips, she figured he might like to finish the job. Besides, he'd do a lot better than she would.

Danita closed the gap between them. "Do you want to help?"

He licked his lips. "I don't know where to begin."

That was such a silly thing to say, but it helped calm her. "There are only two choices, you know."

Griffin reached out and pulled her closer, and his touch ignited her. As afraid as she'd been to make love with him in the past, this felt right. He reached behind her back and unhooked her bra. Instead of taking if off, he pressed his face against her chest, and the pressure soothed every cell of darkness inside her.

He groaned and then slowly ran his hands down her back, causing ripples of pleasure to trip up her spine. She clasped his head and held him close, enjoying his woodsy scent and the rough pads of his fingertips on her skin.

"Danita, what you do to me," he panted.

She wanted to tell him that she was experiencing a rebirth too, but the words wouldn't form. He leaned back and finished lowering her bra straps. To her surprise, he kept his eyes closed. It was almost as if he wanted her to decide what he saw. Her love for him bloomed even more. "You can look."

His eyes sprung open, and his lips parted once more. "You are so delicious."

A second later, his lips were on one breast, sucking and licking. It tickled and hurt a little at the same time, but man, did it feel amazing. Shards of desire rushed through her so hard that she wanted to straddle him.

Hell, why not do that?

She lightly pushed him back so she could climb on his lap. Griffin's fingers tightened on her butt, possibly to keep her from slipping or maybe because he was working hard to keep control. He moved his mouth from one side of her chest to the other. Without meaning to, Danita let a moan escape as he flicked and licked her hard nubs. For the first time in a long time, Danita was safe—safe in his arms and safe from any darkness reaching her. Griffin was her savior.

Not worrying about any kind of negative reaction from him, she allowed herself to let go. Danita ground her hips against his cock and pressed her chest against his lips, while she dragged her hands down his back. She didn't want him to stop, but she needed him naked.

She leaned over his back, grabbed the hem of his shirt, and tugged it upward.

He leaned back. "Let me help you."

A second later, his shirt landed on the floor. This was the first time she'd seen his chest, and it set a fire inside her. She could only imagine what the rest of him looked like. "Wow."

He smiled. "Trust me, there's more to see than a chest."

She couldn't wait.

Chapter Eleven

ONE MINUTE, DANITA was straddling Griffin, and the next he'd placed her on her back on the bed.

"Gotta get rid of these," he said. As if he was performing some big reveal, he turned around and dragged down his pants. Either he wasn't wearing any underwear or else he'd taken them off when he took off his pants. "Oh, shit," he said as he stepped out of his jeans, keeping his back to her.

"What?"

"I don't have any condoms. I wasn't exactly thinking I'd need them."

"Don't worry. I'm on the pill."

He twisted partially around and tossed her a sympathetic smile. "At least one of us is prepared." Griffin chuckled and then stepped out of his pants.

"Come here," she said with a boldness she hadn't heard in her voice in a long time.

When he faced her, wells of lust shot up her throat so hard Danita thought her heart would stop beating. Whoa. She couldn't help but stare at his big cock, and all she could think of was that there was no way he'd fit inside her.

"Don't worry, my little mate. After I finish with you, my dick will slip in with no problem."

The man could read minds? It didn't matter. She trusted him. "Okay."

Gone was her confidence but not her desire. She scooted over on the unmade bed to give him room. He placed a knee on top and crawled toward her, looking like a lion on the hunt. She opened her arms, and he stretched out next to her.

Danita waited a beat for him to pull her to his chest and kiss her, but he seemed to be waiting for her to make the first move. Deciding to satisfy her curiosity, she grabbed his dick. Never did she expect his rust colored scales to flash like a light show. She let go. "What happened?" she asked.

"You happened. When I'm excited, my scales flash, my eyes turn teal, and my teeth sharpen, along with a host of other things. Dragon shifters can't always control how their body reacts, especially when we are around our mate."

In a way, she felt sorry for him. "Is there anything I can do to help?"

He chuckled. "Trust me, you are doing plenty already. Just be yourself and do whatever you want."

His permission freed her. Danita dragged down her panties and tossed them off to the side. Griffin immediately reached out and cupped her between her legs. She couldn't believe how much his strong, powerful fingers turned her on. When he slipped a finger inside her, she rolled onto her back again and spread open her legs, wanting more. Nothing before had caused such wantonness. If she doubted Griffin was her mate, this ended it.

He inhaled deeply. "You are driving me crazy," he said.

"You should be me."

"I like this sassy side of you."

"Is that so?" She opened her arms, and he rolled on top of her, supporting himself with his elbows.

A second later, he dipped his head and kissed her. Their tongues tangled in a delicate dance of exploration. Danita wanted all of him—or rather she needed all of him. That one kiss poured a ton of white light into her, healing her from the inside out.

As much as she loved the kisses and the licks, she'd run out of patience. She needed his cock now. Not sure how to show him short of grabbing it—which was rather impossible with him on top of her—she lifted her hips and wiggled them.

Griffin closed his eyes and broke the kiss. "Hang on a moment. I'm afraid my teeth might cut you."

It took a second for her to understand. When he parted his mouth, his teeth had sharpened. His dragon was turned on.

"Take me."

"I need a bit more time." When Griffin slid between her legs, she inhaled. No man's mouth had ever been there before. Having Griffin being the first would be wonderful though. He widened her legs and licked her.

"Oh, holy hell. That is amazing."

"What's to come will be even better. I promise." As if she hadn't said anything, he continued to suck on her clit.

Just when she thought her insides would explode, he slipped a finger inside her, forcing Danita to grab the sheets and hold on for dear life. The tender loving continued relentlessly until he cupped her breast. The added touch did her in.

"Oh, yes!" she yelled as her orgasm claimed her.

Griffin crawled higher and nuzzled her neck. She stiffened. "I'm not going to bite you," he said.

Her muscles relaxed. While the idea of becoming his mate was attractive, she wasn't ready for that right now. What she was ready for was making love to Griffin. To show him, she ran her hands down his back. The texture was a bit strange, but she'd heard dragon shifters often formed scales temporarily when they were excited. She slipped her arms under his arms, enabling her to reach his butt.

"Oh, my," she said as she squeezed his buns of steel. "They're so hard."

He huffed out a laugh. "I'm glad you like them, but are you ready for something even harder?"

Danita loved this light-hearted side. "Absolutely."

Their lips locked once more as his cock found her entrance. To her delight, her slickness allowed him to slide right in—until he was halfway, that was. It quickly became clear he was just too big. Griffin must have understood what to do, because he slipped out and then tunneled in again. This time, her body accommodated his size. The stretching and his demanding presence had her heart lodged in her throat but only for another few seconds.

Her therapist told her to breathe deeply when she was out of her element, so Danita did just that, and the relaxing effort helped. Griffin slid his hands up to her face and held still for a moment.

"Are you okay?" he asked.

He must have seen the slight panic in her eyes.

"I am now." To show him how much she wanted this, Danita planted her feet on the mattress and pressed her hips upward.

Griffin grunted. All at once his body lit up from the inside, his teeth sharpened, and the colors in his eyes were a sight to see. As if an outside white light entered her body, Danita let go of all of her fears and grabbed hold of his shoulders. What happened after that was almost lost in all of the euphoria raining down on her. They kissed, touched, and stroked each other while she met his thrusts one for one. Danita wasn't going to be passive ever again. She wanted Griffin, and she wanted all of him.

He slid his lips off her mouth and dragged them down her chin and then over to her shoulder blade. He lightly sucked on her skin and then kissed her from neck to the top of her arm. His tenderness soothed any beast that had ever been inside of her before.

She might have been able to hold off her second climax had he not reached between them and pressed on her clit. The combination of his warm body on hers, his lips on her skin, and his hard cock hammering into her, unraveled her. With something that sounded like a scream, Danita inhaled and embraced the waves of orgasmic pleasure.

Griffin must have been waiting for her to release, because he let loose a moment later. When she caught her breath, she hugged him hard. "Thank you."

He lifted his head and dragged a knuckle down her cheek. "I should be thanking you. From the moment I saw you, I knew you were my mate. I also knew you weren't ready to be intimate with me back then. I'm so glad you are now."

Danita had wondered how hard it had been for him to keep his distance. It had been the right thing to do since she had been such an emotional mess for so long. "I know, but I was ready this time."

Griffin kissed her, and the wealth of emotions welled up inside her again. "If I don't stop, I'll want to go again, and you need a break."

"While I'm tempted to continue, you're right."

Griffin slipped out. He left the room and returned a minute later with a wet towel and handed it to her.

"Thanks." No man was more considerate. To her surprise, she wasn't embarrassed about cleaning up in front of him. When she was done, he grabbed the towel and wiped himself clean.

"I'll toss this in the tub, and then help you close that suitcase."

STAYING WITH GRIFFIN the past few days had been wonderful, not only because of their amazing lovemaking, but because of the sense of calm that had enveloped her. There was something about Griffin that soothed her soul. Even her daily life had changed. For the last five months, she'd had the sense that someone was following her, but no longer. Now, Danita doubted that anyone had ever been watching or in wait for her. Stress had caused her to react the way she had, and she couldn't be happier that the paranoia had finally disappeared.

Danita had planned to go into work with Griffin just like he had suggested, but just her luck, she'd been called in for her temporary job. To her delight, even when she was away from him, she didn't have the sense that anyone was out to get her. It wouldn't be long before she said her goodbyes to Dr. Aminor.

"Can you file these too?" her temporary boss asked as she placed a pile of folders on Danita's desk.

"Sure."

She just needed to alphabetize them and then store them in the file cabinet according to last name. Easy enough. She was halfway through her chore when her body locked up and her vision grayed out. Oh, no. She grabbed hold of the file cabinet, fearful she might pass out. This had only happened one other time when she'd had a premonition about Greer, Griffin's sister. Instead of fighting the dark sensations coursing through her like she had the last time, she decided to embrace them and see where they led. If Griffin was in some kind of trouble, she couldn't ignore the warning.

Darkness surrounded her, and the smells of dampness, mold, and cold permeated her. Loud clanging sounds rose up from deep below. Below what? What was she seeing? As if she was having some kind of out-of-body experience, she leaned forward. What looked like men wearing helmets were moving slowly below her. Torches flared, and open carts were moving on rails. In the corner, what she thought was a woman glanced upward. For a split second, Danita imagined her to be Wendy, but that had to be wishful thinking. Or was it? What was this place? Figuring it out might be important.

Before she could decide where to direct her thoughts, a well of panic grabbed her. Someone had spotted her and was shouting at her. She had to get out of there. Danita knew this wasn't real, that she couldn't actually be seen or heard, but the urge to run was strong. She turned around to take off, only to find she was in some kind of maze and couldn't get out. Danita closed her eyes for a moment to block out the images. When she opened them, she was in the fresh air. It was dark outside. Very dark. But the crisp air helped calm her rapidly beating heart. Other than a sliver of moon and some stars, there was nothingness. She needed to figure out what this place was, but all she could make out were tall mountains in the shape of craggy cones looming over her.

"Danita?" a woman's voice asked. Oh, shit.

Shaking herself out of her trance like state, she shut the file cabinet drawer and turned around. "Yes?"

"Are you okay? I've been calling your name."

"Sorry. I was focused on alphabetizing these files." Danita tapped the folders. She certainly wasn't about to say she was having some kind of premonition. "I'm almost done."

Her boss seemed to believe her. She nodded and walked away. For the next hour, Danita focused only on her job and not on what she'd seen in her head. The question that kept bombarding her was what had she really seen? At first glance it could have been some kind of mining operation. Because she'd been determined to learn about Malpan and his mine, she might have merely conjured that up.

For the rest of the afternoon, Danita struggled with the meaning of her vision. As much as she wanted to find these oddly shaped mountains and this underground mine—and maybe even her cousin—she understood she was ill equipped to do so. Her only hope was to elicit help from Griffin.

Too bad she had another hour of work left. She swore the clocks had stopped because it seemed like an eternity before five rolled around. The boss said she'd call tomorrow if Danita's help was needed.

When it was finally time to leave, Danita kept an eye out for anything strange as she rushed to her car, but she spotted nothing out of the ordinary. She jumped in the front seat and locked the doors. When Danita arrived at Griffin's beautiful condo building, she parked underground and took the elevator to the sixth floor. Thankfully, Griffin had added her to the eye scanner, so entering was easy.

Living in his place was such a joy. Not only was it safe, his home was clean and luxurious. Yes, it could use a woman's touch, but she wasn't going to suggest they redecorate any time soon.

As much as she wanted to call Griffin and ask him to come home so she could talk about the premonition, she didn't want to disturb him. To bide her time until he returned, she decided to make him dinner. Danita loved to cook but didn't do it very often. Cooking for one was depressing.

When she looked in the refrigerator for what he had, she was disappointed. Because she didn't feel like going to the store, she cobbled together enough ingredients for an omelet. After setting out the bowls and pans, she went back to the living room to wait.

She had no idea what Griffin's reaction would be when she told him about the potential mine, but she hoped he'd at least want to investigate.

Chapter Twelve

GRIFFIN HAD BEEN putting out fires all day, trying to figure out a way to cut some costs at the copper mine in order to compete with Malpan while still making a profit. It had been a tough go of it these last few weeks.

A knock sounded on his office door, and he glanced up. It was Logan.

"Aren't you going home? It's after five in case you lost track of time," his brother said. "Thought you might like to know."

"Oh, shit. Thanks." Griffin tossed down his pen. "These falling sales are kicking our butts."

"Tell me about it. Any progress on finding out the location of this mythical underground mine that is powered by slaves?" His brother wasn't totally convinced it existed, though he admitted the proof was mounting that it might.

"No, but after finding those ten captured men in the cave, I have no doubt it's somewhere." Griffin's cell rang, and he held up a finger for Logan to stick around. "What do you know? It's Anderson. Hopefully, Arthur Gonzalez talked." Griffin swiped the accept button. "Hey. Can I put you on speaker? Logan is with me."

"Sure."

"Go ahead."

"One of my men spoke with Gonzalez, but he said he couldn't tell whether those names were the men he delivered to Malpan or not. He still claims that when Marty had captured them, they were in their animal form."

"Basically, if he does know, he's not talking," Griffin said.

"Marty was a shifter, so he'd have been able to identify them as such. As a businessman, he wouldn't just pick any random shifter, even if they were of the right age and lacked family in town that might report them missing. Since they couldn't tell by looking at a man what kind he was, Marty and Stick would have followed them. Capturing a dragon shifter, or even a bear shifter, would have caused a shit ton of problems—collar or no collar." Too bad both of these men were dead.

"You have a point. I'll press him further, but it might be a dead end."

"Thanks for trying."

"You bet," Anderson said right before he hung up.

Griffin put his phone away. "That sucks." He pushed back his chair and stood. "I need to get back to Danita."

"How is she doing?"

"Better. She is a little afraid that someone might come after her like they did Wendy since we've been asking questions."

"She has a point," Logan said.

"That's why I asked her to stay with me." He held his breath, waiting for Logan to tell him it was too soon.

A grand smile filled his brother's face. "That's great. Why didn't you tell me? I knew you were dating, so this is the next logical step."

"I didn't ask sooner because I feared Danita would freak. Admitting I'd failed again wasn't something I wanted to talk about."

"I see your point, but I'm glad she agreed."

"Me too."

"So how is that going?" The glint in his brother's eye was unmistakable.

"We've joined forces so to speak."

Logan burst out a laugh. "You go, bro. I'm happy for you."

"Same here, but I might have an unhappy mate if I keep her waiting much longer."

"Agreed."

They walked out together, and Logan locked up the building.

They shifted and headed back toward the condo. Griffin lived on the sixth floor whereas Logan lived on the eighth. Once they landed, Griffin raced down the four flights to his mate. As soon as he stepped into the hallway, waves of lust slammed into him. He had it bad. Real bad.

He knocked on the door and then used the eye scanner to get in. He liked to warn Danita that he was the one entering. "Hi, it's me."

"Hey."

Shit. She sounded worried. When he entered the room, she jumped up, rushed over to him, and gave him a hug. Wow. Never in his wildest dreams did he think he'd be received like that. "As much as I love the reception, I sense something is wrong." He leaned back. "Tell me."

"Why don't you clean up first? I'm making us dinner. Then I'll tell you."

If that was what she wanted, he'd be happy to oblige. "Sure. I won't take long."

Something was troubling her, and Griffin didn't like it. He wanted to hug her and kiss her until she unwound, but for now, he'd do as she asked. After stripping, he jumped in the shower and washed as quickly as possible, all the while listening for any signs of distress. He couldn't wait until they mated. Then he'd be able to sense when something was bothering her.

When he finished washing, he dried off and threw on some clean clothes. As soon as he stepped into the living room, the aroma of eggs cooking and coffee filled the air, and his stomach grumbled. "Smells divine. I didn't know you could cook."

She chuckled. "An omelet hardly tests my true abilities."

"If I had known I'd be coming back to a home cooked meal, I would have finished up my work sooner." Okay, that sounded bad. "But maybe not today. I was swamped with stuff."

"Everything okay?" she asked with a lot of concern in her voice.

If this was what life would be like in the future, he couldn't wait to get started—but only when Danita was ready. "Other than the fact Caspian Mines is bleeding red in our sales of copper, yes."

"Aren't you in charge of sales?"

"Yes, and therein lies the problem."

He explained what his customers had said about Malpan giving them cheaper prices.

She spun around. "That proves it. He has to be using slaves in his mine."

"For now, I'm going with that theory too."

She placed the food on two plates and carried them over to the table. "Sit down, please," she said.

"Can I help?"

"I've got this."

Griffin liked her confidence. True to her word, Danita returned with some toppings for the omelets and then coffee a minute later. He scarfed down the first few bites. "This is amazing by the way."

She grinned. "They are just eggs."

"Eggs that you made. That is what makes them special."

"You are sweet."

Griffin smiled, happy that he'd brought some lightness to his mate. When they finished eating, he insisted on cleaning up while Danita sat in the living room and relaxed. When he was done, he sat next to her. "Tell me what is troubling you."

She inhaled deeply and pressed her lips together. Clearly, this was not going to be easy for her. "I had another premonition."

His pulsed spiked. "Like the one you had for Greer?" Had it not been for Danita's vision, his sister might have been seriously injured or possibly killed when she battled with the Royal Guards.

"Yes, just like that."

"Tell me what you saw and leave nothing out."

She explained about suddenly appearing in what she believed was a mine. "It had to be one, what with the helmets, the carts carrying rocks, and everything."

"How many men did you see?"

"It was hard to tell, but a lot. I know this was probably wishful thinking, but I swear I saw Wendy."

"Wendy? How far away were you?"

Her shoulders slumped. "Probably too far to see anything clearly. It wasn't like things were all that real. I mean, I was looking down at these men from a balcony."

"There are no balconies in mines—at least not in the ones the Caspians have."

"I know. I've only had two premonitions, so I can't be sure how accurate they are."

Danita seemed so convinced that what she saw actually existed that he wanted to believe her. "What happened next?"

"I had this feeling of being watched, so I ran, only there was nowhere to go."

He couldn't imagine being trapped like that. "Did you come out of your premonition at that point?"

"Not yet. I found myself outside for no reason." She explained about the mountains that were shaped like cones. "Have you ever come across anything like those before?"

"No. I wish I had, but that doesn't mean they don't exist. I'll ask Logan to do a topographical search for that kind of land structure."

She clasped his hand. "Thank you for believing me."

He stroked her face. "Why shouldn't I? You've never been wrong."

Griffin pulled her into a hug and held her close. When she moaned, joy spread through him.

"I feel so safe when I'm in your arms," she said.

Those words made this last five-month wait worth it. "That makes me very happy."

Griffin didn't believe for a moment that Danita would just tell him what she knew and then let him handle it. He would be remiss if he didn't remind her of how dangerous it could be if she did something on her own.

"I know I don't have to say this," he began, "but please don't go looking for this mine on your own."

"I won't. It was scary enough when it was just in my mind. That being said, I can take care of myself."

He didn't want to get into this argument again. "How long can you slow time for? A minute? An hour? A day?"

She lowered her gaze. "I don't know. At least a minute."

Shit. "How fast can you run?"

Danita scooted away from him on the sofa. "Okay. I get it. It's dangerous. That's why I won't go looking for the mine."

Now he felt like a cad. "I'm sorry. How can I make it up to you?"

A sly smile crossed her face. "Oh, let me tell you the ways."

Never in a million years would Griffin have imagined that Danita Warren could be a flirt, and he couldn't be happier. "I'm all ears."

THE NEXT MORNING after several rounds of amazing love making, Griffin couldn't wait to see if Logan could find this elusive mine. The sooner he solved that mystery and freed any slaves that might be there, the sooner he could focus his attention on locating Danita's cousin. It seemed to be the last thing to solve before Danita could find peace.

As they finished their breakfast, Griffin asked if Danita had a job today.

"No. I thought I'd go to the office with you, if that's okay."

"That works for me, but you should bring some reading material. My job is often boring." He didn't want her to learn the location of the mine—assuming Logan could even find it, because he knew she would want to search for it.

Once they cleaned up, they drove to the Caspian Mines. He suggested Danita have her car in case she found sitting in his office too dull. Griffin thought Danita would be happy curled up in the chair in his office when he went to speak to Logan. He was wrong.

"I want to see what you do," she said.

"I'm just going to ask Logan to look into finding the area of Tarradon that has those rather pointed mountains you mentioned."

She stood up taller. "I want to come with you."

He didn't have the heart to deny her anything. "Fine."

Once in Logan's office, Griffin asked her to tell Logan about her premonition. Once she finished, Logan asked her a few questions, but she was unable to be more specific about the location.

"I'll do a scan of Tarradon and ask it to match mountains that are like cones. I have read about such structures on Earth. Southern China has some oddly shaped mountains that are made of limestone, dolomite, and gypsum. We don't have dolomite here, but we have the other two materials. That should help narrow the search."

"Thank you so much," she said, clearly pleased that Logan believed her too.

"Give me a bit to look this up. Tarradon is a vast realm. I'll let you know if I find anything that resembles those mountains."

Griffin thanked his brother and left with Danita. As they stepped out, she wrapped an arm around his waist, taking Griffin a bit by surprise at her affection.

"I like Logan," she said.

He chuckled. "I do too, but don't get any ideas. You are my mate, not his."

She punched his stomach with her free hand. "Ouch."

"Serves you right."

They entered his office. "Can you busy yourself until we hear from Logan?" he asked.

"Yes."

For Danita's sake, he hoped that Logan came through.

Chapter Thirteen

LOGAN KNOCKED ON Griffin's office door with a smug look on his face. Danita sat up. "Did you find something?" she asked before Griffin could even open his mouth.

"I may have," he said waving a piece of paper.

"Let's see what you have. Put it here." Griffin pushed back his chair and walked over to the coffee table in front of Danita and cleared a space.

Logan knelt and spread out a map. He'd circled one area. "I have to say I was surprised that there weren't more spots with these kind of odd shaped mountains."

Griffin studied the location. "It's on the edge of Avonbelle Province. It looks like a rather uninhabited area. I wonder how he located this mine, assuming one is there."

"No idea," Logan said. "If we ever find Malpan there, we'll have to ask him."

"Are you going to check it out?" Danita asked, sounding both excited and anxious.

Griffin didn't want to leave her, but she'd probably be happier if he did a quick fly by. "I can do that. I'll look for some equipment or some sign of life. If they put a mine there, the foliage would have been disturbed."

"Take Stone with you," Logan said.

Stone was the youngest Sinclair as well as Logan's assistant. "You don't need him?"

"I can spare him. Knowing you, if you see something, you'll want to investigate. I'd feel better if you had backup."

Griffin didn't need backup, but he knew that Danita would worry less if there were two of them. "Watch Danita for me?"

No surprise, she huffed. "I'm not going to follow you—as if I could."

"Good point."

He leaned over and kissed her. "Be good."

"Always."

That was wishful thinking.

As much as he didn't like leaving her, he trusted Logan to make sure she stayed put. Griffin went in search of Stone and found him in his office next to Logan's.

His cousin looked up and smiled. "Hey. You've been busy."

"I have. You up for a little adventure?"

"Always." Stone pushed back his chair. "Where are we going?"

Griffin placed the map on his desk and told him of Danita's vision. "It could be a wild goose chase."

"Or this could solve our sinking sales problem."

"Way to rub it in."

"Sorry. You know I love the outdoors. I'd rather be flying than sitting behind a desk anytime." He held up a hand. "You don't need to say it. Flying around doesn't pay the bills. Trust me, Dad rubs it in all the time."

Griffin chuckled. That was so Uncle Jackson. "Even if I see mining equipment in the open, I'm not sure we should land. This is a recon mission only."

"You're no fun," Stone said, scrunching up his brows.

"Let's go."

Once outside, they shifted and took off. Even though Griffin had a knack for remembering locations, he'd folded up the map and took it with him. Declan claimed Griffin had a built in GPS, and his cousin might be right.

Griffin inhaled and then shot out a stream of fire. Why? Because he could. It felt good to be doing something that might actually give him results. All those months of waiting for Danita to believe they belonged together had tested his patience. It didn't matter that he and Danita had made love. All was not as it should be in part because he'd failed to find Wendy and that lack of success had dented his confidence. It certainly hadn't made his life any easier when he learned their copper sales had gone in the toilet.

Stone must have sensed Griffin was slowing down, because one minute the two were side by side and the next Stone had shot ahead, showing off by doing a few loops and dives. Being the youngest Sinclair family member, Stone had the tendency to want to try and prove himself. In Griffin's opinion, Stone could do that by keeping alert and not being foolish.

Finding these mountains was important to Danita—and find them he would. He wasn't holding out much hope for locating this copper mine where slaves were being used as workers, but he wanted to locate those geographical anomalies.

Stone came rushing toward him and blew fire close to Griffin's face, shaking him out of his daydreaming once more. Stone screeched, did a loop around him, and headed toward what had to be their limestone mountain peak. Holy shit. They'd found them—or rather Stone had found them.

Griffin's pulse soared. Danita was right. The question was whether she was right about anything else. It only took five more minutes to reach the site, though Griffin did not descend. He believed in studying the scene before rushing in. Stone wasn't as seasoned. His cousin shot straight to an open spot and landed.

Shit. Stone might be ninety, but he was still wet around the ears when it came to common sense. This was the point at which Griffin wished family members had telepathy so they could communicate. Now, he had no choice but to land. When no sentries emerged from this theoretical mine, he decided it might not be bad if he shifted. Stone followed suit.

Griffin couldn't help but stride over to him. "What were you thinking landing?"

"What are you talking about? Look around. There's nothing

here."

"You don't know that, but since there is no mining equipment or trucks to carry back the ore, you might be right."

"Ramsey would kill me if I didn't take back a sample of this mountain side. My brother can do wonders with new rocks. Hell, I wouldn't be surprised if he could polish it into a gorgeous stone."

Griffin couldn't fault his cousin's enthusiasm. "Okay, but be careful."

With a grin, Stone took off to nab a piece of a protruding rock. Griffin had to admit the slender but towering hills were dramatic. In fact, he might even bring Danita here someday to see it in person. She'd be fascinated by all of the green ferns under the tall frenlen trees and how the sunlight accentuated the area. He could even see a picnic in their future.

"Halt," came a command from someone who seemed to appear out of nowhere.

Griffin froze. Shit. Stone was close to this man, a man who was dressed in lightweight sweatpants and a long-sleeved pullover. If he were a sentry, why wasn't he wearing a uniform or carrying any weapon?

Stone lifted his hands as if to shoot fire out of them when the man held up his hand. Without a word, Stone lowered his arms to his side. Okay, that was a little strange.

Griffin strode forward. "We mean no harm. We're here to collect some rock samples." He might as well use Stone's purpose.

"You are Guardians," the stranger stated. It wasn't posed as a question.

Stone glanced back at Griffin. No one but the four sisters knew of their Guardian status. "Why would you think that?"

"I'm Kenton Forrester. I believe you know my sister Fay."

The tension in Griffin's shoulders released. "Yes. You helped my sister Greer when she was in danger."

Kenton smiled, transforming his face into one of almost beauty. "Actually, that was my other sister Meena. I helped Blake find

Greer—or rather I showed him to the portal."

What the hell was he talking about? Neither Blake nor Greer mentioned anything other than spending the night in a cabin. "Portal?"

"I wanted to keep them safe. Both Meena and I thought it best if they stayed in Feyrion, which is our Fey realm."

Fey realm? Really? Why hadn't he heard about this other hidden realm before? Or was this guy talking crap? His gut told him this man was legit. To be fair, Griffin hadn't known about the dark and light realm that Angelique came from either, so maybe there were more realms than even his family had been aware of. Right now, Griffin had other issues to deal with—like finding a cave where they mined copper using slave labor. "Whatever. Why are you here?"

"Stone is a little headstrong. He was about to hit a tripwire." He turned to Griffin's cousin.

"How did you know my name?" Stone asked.

Kenton smiled and tapped his temple. "I know a lot of things. Stand back, and I'll show you."

Without saying a word, Stone moved out of the way, all the while rapidly searching the ground. Kenton picked up a stone and tossed it to the ground not far from where Stone had been standing. Dirt and rocks exploded in every direction. Both Griffin and Stone instantly shifted in order to protect themselves.

When the dust settled, Kenton was standing there completely unscathed with not a speck of dirt on him. How was that even possible? "Did you change into your points of light or something?"

Kenton's eyes widened for a moment. "Oh, you mean because I don't seem to have been affected by the blast?"

Obviously that was what he meant. "Yes."

Kenton laughed. "Just so you know, I'm not a fairy. I can't turn into light."

"But you're Fay's brother."

"My mother is a Fairy, but my dad is a Fey. There is a big difference. I can't fly around like my sisters can either. I have other talents, but we can discuss them at a later date. Right now, I suggest you two get out of here."

Griffin wasn't going to go without a good reason. "Do you know who made the explosive device?"

Kenton twisted toward the mountain. A small tremor rippled across the ground as if an army was headed toward them. That didn't sound good. Maybe it would be smart to return for reinforcements. Before Griffin could ask any more questions, the Fey disappeared. What the hell?

Griffin turned to Stone. "Let's get out of here."

"Hell, no. We need to investigate."

Scraping rocks sounded nearby where the tremor had originated. To him, it implied someone was about to appear, possibly with guns. Not that bullets would kill them, but they were always painful and took a lot out of his dragon to heal him. "There's no time. They're coming."

Not wanting to have a debate, he shifted and soared upward. Griffin doubted that whoever was responsible for the explosion would have much more than a couple of guns, but he didn't want to wait around and find out. Stone swore but then shifted too. He took off after Griffin.

He couldn't blame his cousin for wanting to check things out. Had it not been for Kenton's warning, Griffin would have let his curiosity get the best of him. He figured if this was the place of the underground mine, it would still be there in a few hours when they returned with the force of the Guardians.

DANITA WAS IN the break room pouring herself a cup of coffee when her cell rang. At first, she thought it might be Griffin, but when she checked the screen, she didn't recognize the number. "Hello?"

"Danita, it's me, Wendy."

Danita stumbled backward. Had she not hit the counter, she

might have fallen. "Wendy! Where are you? Are you all right?"

"Yes." The fact her voice shook implied that wasn't totally true. "I need you to listen carefully. You have to get in your car and head out of town. Keep your phone with you. I will call you periodically with directions on where to find me."

"Of course I'll come, but why can't you tell me now?"

"I just can't. Trust me, okay?" Her voice shook.

"Sure. Griffin should be here any minute. I want him to come with me."

"No! You can't tell anyone."

"Why?"

"Just do it. Please? For me?"

Clearly, Wendy was being held captive against her will. While she didn't say what would happen if Danita didn't do as she asked, she bet it would have consequences. "Of course. I'm leaving now."

Her stomach nearly revolted. While Danita was thrilled that Wendy was still alive, this had to be a trap. However, the moment she spotted her cousin, she'd slow down time, grab Wendy, and leave. Yes, that could work.

Logan. Shit. She told him she was getting a cup of coffee. He'd come to investigate in five minutes if she didn't return. That meant she'd have to slow down time around him too so he wouldn't alert Griffin. The problem was that she had no idea how long she could keep the spell going—especially when she wasn't around. Even ten minutes head start would be helpful though.

Griffin and Stone had headed out to find the limestone mountains. Twenty minutes there, fifteen to search, and twenty minutes back, meant they might return any minute now.

With her hot coffee in hand, she returned to Logan's office where he was on the phone. Happy he wasn't paying attention, she set her coffee on the table and then inhaled. She could do this. No, it wasn't for the best of reasons, but she had to save her cousin.

Logan hung up and then turned his attention to his computer. Good. With a sweep of her hand, she said her chant. Logan froze.

Without waiting to see how long her spell would last, she rushed back to the break room, grabbed her purse, and ran out the front door.

It was time to save Wendy.

Chapter Fourteen

A S GRIFFIN AND Stone arrived back at the Caspian Mines, he spotted Danita leaving. Shit! Hadn't he told Logan to keep an eye on her? Or was she terminally bored and needed to get some air. He might have thought the latter, except that he and Stone hadn't been gone even an hour.

They both landed and then shifted. "Wasn't that Danita's car?" Stone asked.

"Yes. She's supposed to have stayed put." Damn woman never could keep out of trouble.

It was possible she'd received a call to go into work. After all, she did work for a temp agency. Before he took off after her half-cocked, he wanted to check in with Logan.

When they stepped into his brother's office, Logan was staring at his computer as if he was frozen. "Logan?"

It took a second before his brother moved. "You're back! Did you find the mountains?"

"We did."

"It was so freaking cool," Stone said as he pulled up a chair, spun it around, and straddled it.

He was halfway through detailing what happened, when Griffin had to stop him. "Before we finish our story, where did Danita go?"

The blank look on his brother's face scared him. "She was here a second ago. She's probably in the bathroom. Her coffee is still on the table."

"I just saw her drive out of here."

Logan stilled. "Are you sure?"

"Yes, I'm sure." He had even sensed her when he flew over her car.

"Shit. I must have been so focused that I didn't even see her leave the office."

Griffin turned to Stone. "Tell him the rest of the story. I'm going to make sure Danita is okay."

"But we need to get back to the mine right now," Stone said.

Logan pushed back his chair and stood. "You found the mine? Why didn't you say so?" He glanced between both of them.

"We never actually saw the mine. Look, it's complicated. I have to see if Danita is okay. In the meantime, why don't you two round up a few Guardians and head on over there. Just be careful of any explosives." Griffin held up his hand. "Stone will tell you about it." He faced his cousin. "Do you remember the way?"

"Do *I* remember the way? I'm insulted. Remember, I was the one who found the damn mountains in the first place."

"Sorry. I'm not thinking straight. I'm worried about Danita."

Logan made a shooing motion. "Go. We've got this."

"As soon as I figure out what my mate is doing, I'll head on out there. If I get there first, I'll wait."

"Make sure you do, but don't worry," his brother said. "We can handle it."

With things more or less under control, Griffin rushed out and shifted. In the ten minutes he'd spent with Logan and Stone, Danita shouldn't have made it to town yet. She'd be easy to find.

A minute later he spotted her, but only because his body had reacted. Danita was sitting in traffic on the edge of town. Because he had no idea where she was going, he circled high overhead. When the line of traffic eased up, Danita continued down the main street. However, when she headed north without stopping, Griffin's concern grew. There was nothing out there but the forest where that Changeling from Earth had attacked her.

Shit. Where was she going? As much as Griffin wanted to land in front of her and demand she stop, she'd had enough people in her life telling her what to do. No, for the sake of their future relationship, he had to let her see this through. If she did anything even remotely dangerous, he would interfere.

Out of the corner of his eye, he spotted four Guardians heading toward those limestone mountains. The temptation to follow them was strong, but his protective need to watch over Danita was stronger.

Had he not been able to sense Danita when he flew above the canopied trees of the forest, Griffin would have landed. When her car popped out of the other side and she kept driving, his confusion grew.

For the next hour, his frustration continued to build. When he saw the same four Guardians return from the direction of the mine, he relaxed. Nothing must have been there. While it was possible they were returning for more backup, that wasn't anyone's style. Unless more than ten highly trained dragons were there, they wouldn't have thought they needed more help.

Perhaps it had been his imagination that he'd heard what sounded like pounding feet coming from deep underground. Come to think of it though, he remembered Stone saying he felt the tremors too. Hell. For all he knew, Kenton Forrester had set the explosive device because he didn't want them to discover something—like what? Another portal to his Fey realm? Malpan might not have been involved at all.

Hoping all was well, Griffin continued to keep watch over Danita. She could only drive for so long without stopping for fuel. For that to happen, she'd need to take a side road to another town. Then he'd confront her.

When she turned right and headed in the direction of the limestone mountains, Griffin's pulse soared. She couldn't be going there. She claimed she had no idea where they were. Had she been lying to him all along? It seemed highly improbable, but he'd been fooled before.

Needing to focus, he swooped lower and cloaked himself. If she spotted him, she'd recognize his black scales sprinkled with rust ones. No telling what she'd do then. One thing was certain: she wouldn't be pleased that he'd been hovering overhead.

Fifteen minutes later, she came to a stop on a dirt road because several logs blocked the path. Clearly, they'd been strategically placed there to keep people out. He dipped lower. She cut the engine, pushed open her door, and eased out. As if the logs weren't there, she walked around them and continued, clearly determined to reach her goal.

When the trees thickened, he had no choice but to land and shift. While he couldn't cloak himself in his human form, he could hide behind trees and large rocks. His ability to sense her presence allowed him to have the patience to let her disappear before he went after her, all the while staying out of view.

Eventually, she arrived at the open area where he and Stone had first landed. Griffin expected her to stop and admire the view, but instead, she walked toward one of the towering mountains and only stopped when her cell rang. He wasn't close enough to hear the conversation, but it might have been a wrong number because she disconnected seconds later.

Griffin held his breath that whoever had set the first tripwire hadn't replaced it with another explosive.

Since there was a large open space between them, he had to wait until she was closer to the base of the mountain before he made his move. Just when he was about to dart out from behind a tree, Danita disappeared right into the mountain. His heart plummeted to his gut. Griffin shifted, cloaked, and flew across the field. Either she had the ability to teleport or someone had snatched her from behind and had been too quick for him to see.

Griffin landed close to where he'd seen her last, shifted, and then searched the area on foot. All he saw was some large rocks. There were no other paths leading to or away from it.

Wait a second. A slight gap existed where someone could have squeezed through—someone small like Danita but not him. Shit.

A hundred scenarios raced through his mind. Even though it would only take him fifteen or twenty minutes to fly back and get help, he didn't want to leave her. Griffin pressed his face to the small opening and spotted her standing about thirty feet from the rock wall doing nothing. Relief cascaded through him that she appeared to be okay—and alone. How she knew to go inside was anyone's guess. All that appeared to be in front of her was darkness. Clanging sounds and a few shouts finally reached him. Something or someone was in there.

He was about to shout her name when Danita waved a hand and then spun around. Griffin ducked. Shit. If she spotted him, she'd be royally pissed. Thinking she was heading out, he shifted and soared straight up. He cloaked himself, believing she'd never know he was there.

Sure enough, Danita slipped through the crack, turned, and half-jogged and half walked back to her car, never looking over her shoulder. As much as he wanted to land and hug her because she was unharmed, now wasn't the time. Something must have spooked her. Respecting her reaction, he let her reach the safety of her car. Once she returned to town, they'd have a talk—boy would they. Griffin would tell her that he'd followed her, so she'd understand that denial was futile.

As soon as Danita climbed into her car, he was able to relax. She did a U-turn and headed back the way she came.

AS GRIFFIN REPLAYED in his mind how Danita had driven straight to the tall mountains and then ducked into what might have been a mine, he had become more agitated by the minute. When he did finally speak with Danita, he hoped she'd have a good explanation for what the hell had happened. To think she'd promised him she wouldn't leave the Caspian Mines. He'd been a fool to trust her.

Once she pulled into his condo parking garage, Griffin landed on the roof, shifted, and took the elevator to his floor and beat her there. Inside the condo, he paced. He wanted to keep his cool, but fear for her safety brought his anger to the surface.

Footsteps sounded and then the door handle twisted. While it would be less confrontational if he were in the kitchen pretending to grab a beer, he couldn't wait. She pushed open the door and halted.

"What are you doing home?" she asked.

"Stone and I got back early. What about you? I thought you were going to stay with Logan for the day. It's only four."

"Yeah, about that." She avoided his gaze as she slipped off her jacket. "I talked to Wendy."

His anger almost disappeared. "Is she okay? Where is she? Tell me."

Griffin motioned that they sit down, but Danita remained standing. "I got a call while I was making coffee in the break room. It was Wendy. I honestly don't even remember exactly what she said. I was too excited to learn she was alive." Danita threaded her fingers together.

"Where was she? Is she safe?"

Danita inhaled. "I don't know. I think someone is keeping her captive.

"I don't understand."

"I spoke with Wendy for less than a minute. I could tell she was calling under duress, but I couldn't ask her about her captor. She told me to head out of town and that she would contact me when I was on my way to direct me where to go."

"Why didn't you call me?"

She lifted her head and looked him right in the eye. "She said I couldn't tell you. I had the sense her life was on the line."

That was a lame excuse. "I could have flown overhead and cloaked myself. Her captor never would have known."

"Do you answer your phone when you're in your dragon form?"

She had a point. "Did you try to contact me?" He pulled out his cell to check for a message, but found none.

"No."

Griffin stepped toward her. "Did you really think this guy—who could have been Malpan—would have handed Wendy over to you just like that? Did he say what he wanted?"

She crossed her arms over her chest. "No."

Griffin didn't want to make matters worse for her, but Danita had to understand that she couldn't just go out on her own. "So did you do as she asked?"

"Yes."

He was impressed with her honesty. "And?" Extracting information out of her was next to impossible.

"I drove to the mine."

"So there is a mine there?" Then why hadn't the Guardians found it? Or had they? He hadn't spoken with Logan yet. Griffin didn't want to believe that Kenton Forrester was in cahoots with Malpan.

"Yes."

"Danita! Stop with the one-word answers."

When he blinked, she was gone. He spun around and found her sitting at the dining room table with a steaming cup of tea in front of her. She looked up and briefly smiled.

"I'm sorry, but I had to slow down time. You have no idea what I'm going through. It was terrible. Yelling won't help us find Wendy."

When her bottom lip trembled, his anger disappeared. "I am sorry." Griffin pulled up a chair across from her.

"I'll tell you the rest, but you have to promise not to be so judgmental."

She was asking the impossible. "I'll try but no promises."

Danita blew on her hot tea and then took a sip. "Wendy called me about four times while I was driving. I swear her captor had to have been tracking me. Otherwise, how did she know exactly where I was?"

"Fuck. When you worked at Malpan's office, did you ever leave your purse in the open?"

"I can't remember. Maybe, but there was no way Malpan would have known who I was at the time."

"I wouldn't be so sure."

She wagged a finger at him. "We were asking questions. I suppose someone could have put a tracking device on my car."

"I'll check it out. Go on." This man's devious plan was becoming clearer.

"Wendy led me right to the mine, even telling me the dirt road would be blocked. Before I reached the entrance, she called me again, detailing how to find the mine opening. I tried to ask her questions about her captor, but she cut me off. When I reached the space in the rock wall, I was surprised anyone other than a woman could squeeze through."

"What did you see? I take it Wendy was not there?"

"I'm not sure. When I walked in, there was an elevator on the right and an overlook in front of me. It was really dark in there. It was just like my premonition, which was really scary. I peeked over the edge, and I swear I saw Wendy down below, tied up."

His mind spun with what they should do next. "Did anyone call again?"

Danita looked up. "No, in part because I got this really creepy feeling of not being safe anymore, so I slowed down time. I waited until everyone was still before I hightailed it out of there. I really didn't know how long they would have stayed that way, so I removed the stoppage once I reached the edge of the field. I then ran back to my car and drove straight here."

"I'm happy you had the good sense not to try to find Wendy on your own. Most likely her captor would have had Wendy ask you to take the elevator down to the mining floor, and then he would have kidnapped you too. It sounds like the whole thing was a setup to trap you like Wendy."

She shook her head. "It makes no sense. Why me? Did he know I was looking into his whereabouts?"

"I wish I had the answers. Stone and I found that same mountain, but Kenton Forrester was there."

"Who's he?"

Griffin explained the best he could how Kenton's sisters, as well as Kenton, had helped his family many times. "Had he not shown us the trip wire, it's possible Stone would have been injured."

"That's scary. Did you ask Kenton about the mine?"

"Between the explosion, hearing sounds of rumbling underneath us, and Kenton's warning, we took off before we could ask him. When I returned to Caspian Mines, I asked Stone and Logan to grab a few more men and check it out."

"What did they find?"

"I haven't been back to ask them."

Danita huffed out a sigh. "Oh."

Griffin reached across the table and clasped her hand. "We will get Wendy back."

"How? You can't fit through that small slit in the rock to look for her."

"I have some ideas. We will worry about all this in a bit just as soon as I check in with Logan." Danita winced, and Griffin sat up straighter. "What is it?"

"It's nothing."

"It's not nothing. You always say that. Tell me. Please. If we are going to be together, there can be no secrets between us." Okay, he didn't tell her his secret that he'd followed her to the limestone mountain, but now wasn't the time to divulge that.

"It's the darkness. It's getting worse."

Fuck. "Sanditra is dead. How is that possible?"

"I don't know, but it seems that when I do something that isn't for the greater good, my darkness grows."

This really concerned him. "Describe what you did exactly that might have caused this to manifest itself."

"When I followed Wendy's instructions instead of telling Logan or you what I'd found out, I could feel this burning in my body."

"That might have been plain old fear. Besides, you thought it was for Wendy's good to do as she asked."

Danita looked off to the side, her mind obviously spinning. "Okay, it was probably when I slowed down time at the mine in order to escape."

"Which I don't see as bad."

Danita tilted her head. "Maybe, but that ability to slow time is a result of having been with that terrible dark lighter."

"You never had that power before?"

"No!"

There was so much to learn about her. Griffin had to get her help—real help—before Danita was eaten up with darkness. He snapped his fingers. "I have it. Come on." He pushed back his chair.

"Whoa. Where are we going?"

"To the Four Sisters' Pottery shop."

"Weren't they the ones who helped me get out of the Royal prison?"

"In a manner of speaking, yes. When Kaleena returned from being with Sanditra, she possessed some darkness too. The four sisters were able to remove the poison from her body."

"Why didn't you say something before?"

Why hadn't he? "I don't know. Maybe I thought your case might be worse since you were with Sanditra longer. I didn't want to get your hopes up."

Danita slumped. "Oh."

"We have nothing to lose by asking them, okay?"

"Do you think they would help me again?"

"You are my mate, so yes."

"What about Logan? Shouldn't we find out what he learned first?"

"He'll call if they found anything."

Chapter Fifteen

"**D**O YOU THINK you can help her?" Griffin asked Poppy who was biting her lip, her gaze looking everywhere but at Danita.

Magnolia was standing next to them, studying Danita's body. "We can try," Magnolia said. "Why don't you come back to the house? It will be more comfortable there."

Griffin had never heard of any of the Guardians being invited to their inner sanctum before. "That would be nice."

"I need to stay here and mind the store, but Poppy can hopefully help you out," Magnolia said.

Griffin had heard that to be effective, all four sisters needed to work together. Would one sister's abilities be enough to remove so much darkness? He might have said something if he didn't fear it might upset them. They were being nice enough to try.

Poppy led the way. After walking through a workroom, they entered a door that led to a long hallway.

Poppy stopped and faced them. "Griffin, why don't you go into the kitchen and grab something to drink. Slade is in there. He's my mate." She grinned. "He's also a contractor, so you two might have something in common."

"Sure." Apparently, Poppy didn't want him with them when she performed her magic. As long as this sister was able to help Danita, he didn't care, though he wasn't sure what a contractor and a miner would have in common.

Griffin stepped into the kitchen and instantly recognized this man as a fellow dragon shifter. "Hello," Griffin said.

The man turned around and smiled. Griffin held out his hand

and introduced himself. "Griffin Caspian."

"Slade LaMont," Poppy's mate said. "Is my mate doing something special in there?"

"Yes. My mate was subjected to a dark lighter and needs some help."

"Ah. I think that calls for a beer. Want one?"

"You read my mind." Griffin liked this guy.

Slade laughed. "I don't have that talent, but I swear some of the Faiten sisters can do just that."

For the next fifteen minutes, Poppy worked on Danita. With each minute that passed, Griffin became more concerned. Just when he was about to go into the living room to check on them, Poppy and Danita returned. Griffin jumped up. "How did it go?"

Danita's frown and worried brows told it all. "Not good," she said.

"I'm sorry," Poppy said. "There is something inside Danita that I've not dealt with before. It's not the darkness of a dark lighter but that of a dark Fey."

"A dark Fey? I didn't know they existed." Griffin couldn't help but think of Kenton—not that he was a dark Fey—but he might know someone who could help. "Are you familiar with the Forrester family?" Griffin wanted some kind of reassurance that they were as honorable as they seemed.

Poppy smiled. "As a matter of fact, I was just about to suggest you speak with either Kenton or Bevon Forrester. One of them might be able to help."

"You've worked with them before?" Kenton seemed to possess a lot of magic, so perhaps they had interacted.

"I've not worked with them, but I know who they are. You can trust them."

"That's good to know. We'll try them next. Thank you." He turned to Slade. "Nice to meet you."

"Back at you."

He slipped next to Danita and drew her close. "Are you up for a little journey?"

"I'd go anywhere to rid my body of this evil. Five months of therapy didn't help all that much. Hopefully, this will." She turned to Poppy. "I really appreciate you acknowledging that something is wrong, and it's not all in my mind."

"No. Sanditra was definitely evil. We always knew she was bad, but we hadn't interacted enough to realize she wasn't from this realm."

Sanditra must have come to Tarradon through the portal that Kenton spoke of. "I'm curious. How were you able to heal Kaleena then?" Griffin asked.

"She wasn't with Sanditra for long. We were able to take out the poison quite easily in part because Sanditra hadn't given Kaleena a part of her soul like she did with Danita."

"I don't even want to know what that is about," Griffin said.

Danita leaned harder against him. "The whole idea makes me want to puke."

"Go to the Feys. They should be able to help." Poppy pointed to the back door. "If you flew here, you can go out back and take off from there."

"Thank you."

Once they were outside, Griffin worried about Danita. "Are you okay with flying to the middle of the realm now? Or would you rather rest?"

"Are you kidding me? Once I learned about what Sanditra had done to me, all I've wanted is to get it out of me."

"Is it physical?"

She shook her head. "I don't know. For all I know, Sanditra turned her darkness into smoke and blew it into me when I was in a trance. It wasn't as if she operated on me and stuffed something inside. At least I hope that's not what she did. I'm just hoping one of the Feys will know what to do."

He loved her strength. Other than the darkness inside her, he loved everything about her. "Let's go."

Griffin shifted and then picked up Danita. The trip to the eternal flame seemed to take forever, but eventually, the forest appeared. It was close to dark when he landed.

"It's about a twenty-minute hike in," he said. "Can you make it?"

"I'd make it even if I had to crawl."

He leaned over and kissed the top of her head. "I would have carried you."

Wanting to allow Danita time to center herself, Griffin said very little as they headed down the flat, wide path. He figured if she wanted to talk, she would have.

To his delight, when they reached the eternal flame both Kenton and Fay were there, almost as if they were expecting them. He'd met Fay at Birk and Lily's wedding.

"I'm glad you could make it," Kenton said.

"Did Poppy or Magnolia contact you to let you know we were coming?" Griffin asked.

"No, but we suspected you might seek our help," Kenton said.

Danita squeezed his hand. "Oh, sorry," Griffin said. "This is my mate, Danita Warren. She had a run in with a dark lighter a few months back, and even though she is dead, the darkness still resides in Danita. Poppy said the evil is from a dark Fey."

Fay stepped closer, closed her eyes, and then turned into a very small person with wings. Danita squeezed his hand once more. While he didn't sense any fear in her, she appeared to be a bit confused. Fay landed on Danita's shoulder for a moment and then flew off, reappearing as a woman. "I sense the darkness in you."

"Can you get rid of it?"

Fay smiled. "I believe Kenton and I can help you out."

Danita let go of his hand and hugged Fay. "Thank you. What do you need me to do?"

"I'd like both you and Griffin to come to our cabin. I can remove the dark soul in there," Kenton said.

"How?"

Kenton smiled. "It's one of our talents. Don't worry. It's not painful. What was the name of this dark Fey?"

"Sanditra."

"Oh."

Danita looked up at Griffin and then back at Kenton. "Do you know her?"

"Only in death. After she died, I was the one who escorted her dark soul to our realm. We have a place where, shall we say, we retire their darkness. No one can access it ever again."

"I wish you'd have been able to retire her when she was here," Danita mumbled.

"Can we get started?" Griffin asked. The sooner the darkness was out of Danita, the sooner the two of them could mate—assuming she wanted to.

"Of course. Kenton can show you the way to the cabin," Fay said. "Please say hello to your brother and sister for me, Griffin."

"I will." Nessa was the first one to meet Fay and find out another type of person existed. No one in their family really understood the full extent of their powers though.

"This way," Kenton said.

For the next fifteen minutes, they followed him down the rather dark path. Griffin held Danita's hand because her eyesight wasn't as good as his.

Kenton stopped. "We're here."

"I don't see anything," Danita said as she leaned in close.

Griffin didn't either for a moment. Then he spotted a cute log cabin. His sister Greer had described her cabin as rather modern. There must be a lot of cabins around here because this wasn't modern at all, but he liked this one.

"Follow me," Kenton said.

When they stepped inside, Danita smiled. "I love this. It's small but cute."

On one of the walls was a large photo of a flowered field. How perfect. Because she seemed so at peace in a place like this, Griffin would have to see about building a weekend getaway for her closer to Edendale.

"I can work better in the bedroom. Both of you, come on," Kenton said.

Griffin was glad he was invited to see what Kenton was going to do because even though Danita was getting help, his dragon was none too fond of the idea of his mate in a bedroom with another guy. His animal was a particularly protective beast since they hadn't mated yet.

KENTON SAID IT wouldn't hurt, but Danita didn't really believe him. It wasn't the pain she was worried about though, it was whether he would succeed. The fact he understood about Fey souls though gave her hope.

They stepped into a cute bedroom that actually had a king-sized bed with two cushioned high-backed chairs snuggled up against a table. The place couldn't be cozier. The warm pink and green colors were so soothing too. It was almost as if he'd read her mind about her perfect dream bedroom. The small lamp on the side of the bed cast a yellow glow, adding to the calming effect. All that was missing was a little music and maybe a stick of incense.

"Danita go ahead and lie on the bed face up."

She crawled on top, and then used the stack of pillows to support her head. Not wanting to get dirt on the spread, she ditched her shoes. "I'm ready."

Kenton smiled once more. She really liked his non-threatening demeanor. "Close your eyes and go to your safe space."

He sounded a lot like Dr. Aminor. This time when she mentally visited her hillside garden, she pictured Griffin with her. Even though her lids were closed, Danita could see Kenton's shadow hover above her. Griffin would be watching intently and not let anything happen to her. While she couldn't see exactly what he was doing, the heat inside her body seemed to be moving. The sensation wasn't bad, just different.

"I'm going to place my hands on your shoulders," he said right before he did.

Kenton started to hum and then sway. As if a current was going through his hands, his fingers began to vibrate. The pressure increased, and her insides seemed to be lifting. As far as she knew, souls weren't physical, so it wasn't as if he had to open her up to remove it.

Her mouth opened on its own. As much as she wanted to look at what was happening, she didn't. Danita wouldn't do anything to hinder this exorcism, if that was what this was.

What tasted like rancid milk tinged her tongue, but she didn't spit it out or close her mouth. Kenton said something in a language she'd never heard before, and it was as if waves of light began to occupy her body. Joy followed as euphoria filled her. Her body shook for a moment and then her muscles gave way. Her head lolled to the side, and her mind blanked.

Someone shook her. "Danita, are you okay?"

It was Griffin's voice. Her eyelids wouldn't move. In fact, her whole body was unable to engage. She wanted to tell him she could hear him, but nothing worked.

"I'm back. Danita, you can wake up now." That was Kenton. When he touched her cheeks with both of his palms, her eyes flew open.

More energy than she'd experienced in a long time entered her. She sat up and smiled.

Griffin leaned over her. "How do you feel?"

She had to think about it. "Amazing! I feel free, like a heaviness has been taken away. I always felt like I was trudging through mud before but not anymore."

Kenton chuckled. "I'm so happy. I was able to remove all of the evil part that Sanditra had left inside of you as her legacy. It was almost as if she knew her time was up."

"Do I even want to ask what was inside me?"

Kenton shook his head. "It's probably better that you don't. I went to Feyrion and handed her piece of darkness over to the guards who will dispose of it."

She shivered. "That is creepy." The enormity of what Kenton had done finally sunk in. "So, no more darkness?"

"As far as I believe, no, but you'll need to rest. Spend the night here. Tomorrow will be soon enough to return to Edendale a new woman." He turned to Griffin. "I don't expect Danita to experience any kind of setback, but if something seems off, come get us. If you show up at the eternal flame, we'll find you."

Griffin stuck out his hand. "I can't thank you enough."

"Ridding this realm of even another piece of a dark Fey is thanks enough." He bowed and walked out.

Wow. "I can't believe it. I must have been conked out because I don't remember Kenton leaving."

"You were asleep for about a half hour."

"I remember nothing other than heat rising up in my body."

Griffin sat on the bed and she scooted over. "Maybe it's for the best that is all you recall, but I have to admit that it was the longest half hour in my life."

Danita lifted her hand and stroked his cheek. "I love you, Griffin Caspian."

"I've loved you for a long time, Danita Warren."

She smiled. "What are we going to do about this love?"

Griffin stroked his chin. "Hmm. We could rest and see what we feel like in the morning."

That was a dumb idea. "I thought more on the lines of me riding you tonight."

He laughed. "Are you sure you're up for that? You did just have part of your soul removed."

"Sanditra's soul. Mine can finally breathe. It's as if the curtains have been drawn back and the windows opened for the first time in months."

"Then I say let the games begin."

Chapter Sixteen

F OR THE FIRST time in forever, Danita was almost giddy. "I can't believe I'm finally free of the darkness."

Griffin toed off his shoes, climbed onto the bed, and gathered Danita in his arms. His protective warmth soothed all of the hurt she'd experienced in the past.

"I couldn't be happier for you. I would say we're home free, but I know we still have to rescue Wendy."

Oh shit. She jerked out of his arms. "How could I have forgotten? We need to do something now."

Griffin pulled her back down. "It's late. Even if you saw her in the mine, I would imagine her captor would have moved her by now."

She slumped against his chest. "What are we going to do?"

"Tomorrow, I will have a meeting with the Guardians."

"I appreciate that."

She reached behind his head and pulled his face toward her to kiss him, which turned out to be the best one in her memory. Why? No longer did she fear that some of her darkness would enter his body. Thankfully, she was once more her light self—a woman who could enjoy life and just let go.

"Mmm," Griffin said as he leaned back. "You even kiss better now. Damn dark Fey."

She raised her brows. "How do you know I kiss better? You hadn't met me before I was in prison."

He smiled. "I have a good imagination."

"Well imagine this," she said as she grabbed his crotch. As wonderful as it was to hold him in her hand, his jeans prevented her from fully enjoying him. Good thing she could do something about that.

He clamped a hand over hers. "Trust me, my imagination went there a long time ago."

She did love this man. If there was one constant in their relationship, it was that Griffin was always there for her. That, and the sex was amazing. Danita sat up, sprang to the end of the bed, and then straddled him. "These have to go."

Griffin unhooked the waistband and then unbuttoned his jeans. Taking control, Danita leaned over and tugged. Darn. Unless he lifted up, she couldn't remove them.

"Let me," he said with a twinkle in his eye.

He slid his pants and briefs down over his butt. She then finished taking off both of them. "Nice," she said in reference to his amazing cock that was definitely ready to go.

Even though she was clothed, she straddled him, leaned over, and kissed him again. When their tongues intertwined, she rubbed her hips against his burgeoning cock, causing him to moan. Perfect. That was just the response she was looking for. As if he couldn't handle the pressure, Griffin took hold of her hips and held her still. Too bad she was just as affected, but that didn't mean she intended to let him take full control. She had her life back, and Danita wanted to live it to the fullest.

Needing to press her breasts against his naked chest, she sat up and lifted off her shirt. Danita tossed it off the bed not bothering to look where it landed. His eyes turned a beautiful teal that she so enjoyed.

"As much as I love the sexy red bra, it has to go too."

With a quick pinch in back, the bra sprung open. Eager to have his mouth on her, she slipped down the straps, and then discarded the bra in the same direction as her shirt. She'd let him suffer a little longer before she removed her jeans.

Griffin flipped her over.

"I can't keep my hands off you. I need all of you." He unhooked her pants then moved to her ankles and tugged. Her panties snagged in the pants and came off at the same time. Talk about a time saver.

Once he added her clothes to the already mounting pile, he removed his shirt. Now that they were both naked, they could more fully enjoy each other. Nice.

Danita ran her nails down his chest and then latched onto his hard shaft.

He lifted her fingers off of him. "None of that until I've tasted you. I want to see if it's better without the darkness."

"The darkness was on the inside, silly."

"You never know."

Griffin slid down, spread her legs wide, and lowered his head. The first lick had her practically rising off the bed. Without all of the depression and anxiety coursing through her, she could embrace every second.

Danita wanted to bend her legs so she could press up with her hips, but he held her down, and his dominance actually turned her on even more. She grabbed his shoulders and squeezed, loving the way his muscles bunched and pulsed with every bob of his head. His power and obvious desire seeped into her, making her whole once more.

Lust sped through her veins, and she wasn't sure how much longer she could hold out. Griffin let go of one leg in order to palm her breast. When he gently pinched her nipple and sucked hard on the tiny nub, erotic pleasure soared and then spiked. She couldn't have held back her climax if she'd tried. To be honest, even she didn't recognize the sound of the cry that burst forth from her lips.

Griffin stopped and looked up. "Definitely better."

She guessed he was referring to her newfound light. "Let me return the favor. It's only fair."

He held up a hand. "I make no promises."

"I'm willing to take my chances." Excited to see how far she could push him, she knelt next to his cock and took hold. The thickness and strength radiated power. Danita giggled, something she hadn't done in a long time. "I think I can see pulses of light inside."

"That does seem to be what is happening," he said as he sucked in his breath.

Danita pumped her fist a few times before running her tongue along the rim of his cock. Griffin grabbed her arm and exhaled. His eyes were closed, but his breathing had increased. She was getting to him. The real issue was that the more she licked and sucked, the more she wanted to have him inside her. This might be harder on her than on him.

Wanting to taste all of him, she opened her throat and delved down, only to find he was too big. Fisting her hands at the bottom of his shaft, she pumped and licked and loved on him. Only when a shot of cum bubbled up did she stop. Mission accomplished.

"Now for some real fun," she said.

"What are you doing?" Griffin asked as she straddled him.

"This."

She took hold of his cock, aimed, and sunk down. Whoa! Pleasurable waves pulsed through her. When the initial shock wore off, Danita wanted to celebrate her new life—one without darkness and one with Griffin in it.

"Come here, Ms. Light." Griffin pulled her down and kissed her hard.

When he slid his hands from her shoulders to her hips, anticipation soared. The kiss intensified. He slid out and drove right back in, spiking her need. Their previous lovemaking had been amazing, but this even topped that.

With her hands on either side of his head, she lifted up and offered him her right breast. The first suck was intense in part because his teeth had sharpened. "Careful!"

He let go. "Sorry. I got carried away." He closed his eyes for a second and his teeth returned to normal. He must have commanded his dragon to stand down.

Danita wasn't sure she'd ever understand how the dragon-man thing worked, but as long as Griffin could control his animal, it worked for her.

One second she was on top, and the next she was on the bottom.

Danita laughed and then kissed him. This angle might actually be better because now she could run her hands over his head, down his shoulders, and around his back so she could squeeze his butt. Oh, yum. Everything about this man ignited her core.

Returning the kiss, he pumped and thrust, sometimes going fast and at other times withholding the pleasure from her. Two could play at this game. Danita pressed her feet against the mattress and lifted her rear. She met his thrusts with equal fervor. The joining turned wilder and more passionate with each second. Between his intense eye color, his scales flashing rust, and his teeth sharpening, Griffin was close to losing his control.

When he broke the kiss and then nipped at her shoulder, her climax consumed her. Stars burst onto the back of her lids and stole her breath away. Griffin slid his arms under her back and pulled her tight as his orgasm let loose.

Neither said anything for a while, probably because they were trying to come to grips with how totally consuming their lovemaking had been.

"I need to get something to clean us up," Griffin said after a long while.

To her surprise, the one-bedroom cabin had an adjoining bath. He returned with a wet washcloth and cleaned up both of them. Her muscles had all but melted, so when Griffin slid into bed afterward, she was almost asleep.

Danita woke during the night and found Griffin on top of the blankets stark naked. Enough moonlight was streaming through the window to let her see him in all of his glory. Even though he was quietly snoring, she needed to touch him. Most likely he'd wake, so she wanted to make the most of her touch. As she reached out, he grabbed her wrist, smiled, and rolled over to face her.

"How did you know I was about to touch you?" The man would never cease to amaze her.

"You aren't the only one with magic, my dear."

"Is that so? What can you do? You've seen my magic."

"Besides being able to cloak myself in my dragon form?" he asked.

"Yes, though that is impressive."

"Let's see. I can tell one shifter from another even when they are in their human form. I've also been known to do a bit of telekinesis. But my biggest talent is always being aware of you."

He was probably teasing, but she loved it. "We'll have to play hide and seek sometime to test your skills."

His eyes gave a flash of teal. "Once this mess with the mine is over, there are a lot of games I'd like to play with you."

She liked the sound of that. Danita couldn't remember ever seeing Griffin so carefree. He always walked around carrying the weight of the world on his shoulders. "Name one."

"How about light my fire? I have a really big stick you can rub." He grabbed his hard shaft and waved it.

Danita rolled her eyes. "What kind of game is that? Not that I'm against it, mind you."

He pulled her close and kissed her. All thoughts of games disappeared as waves of delight washed through her. Oh, how this man could inflame every cell in her body with one kiss. Clearly, Fate had been right when she decided they belonged together.

Chapter Seventeen

G RIFFIN WAS NOT excited to leave the wonderful cabin in the woods, but there were men to save—not to mention poor Wendy. After they found Kenton at the eternal flame with two of his sisters, Meena and Tally, they thanked him profusely for helping Danita and for letting them spend the night in the cabin.

"If we can do anything for you or your family, please let us know," Griffin said as he shook Kenton's hand.

"It was my pleasure. Safe trip home."

With nothing more to say, he and Danita traveled the path back to the opening at the end of the forest. This time, the sun was shining, and he swore Danita almost glowed. Having the darkness inside her removed made everything so much better.

When they reached the exit, Griffin faced her. "Ready for the flight back?"

"Yes." She twisted back toward the forest. "I'll miss it here."

Griffin stroked her face. "We can come back whenever you want."

"I'd like that."

Whether they could use the cabin was anyone's guess. Griffin shifted, picked up Danita, and headed back to Edendale. This time his heart wasn't heavy.

The hour trip passed quickly. Because it was early, he headed straight to Caspian Mines. He was sure Danita would want to know if they had any news on her cousin. He landed, set her down, and shifted.

"Let's see if the men know anything about the mine and its

occupants," he said.

"I have the sense that whoever is behind this probably moved Wendy. I hope nothing happened to her since I didn't stay around."

"If he wants you for some reason, he'll keep her alive. He might have seen you arrive and then leave. He won't know the reason for you not remaining there," Griffin said.

"Whatever he believes, he won't be pleased."

"So true."

Griffin held open the office door and Danita stepped inside. "I need to apologize to Logan," she said.

"Why?"

"Because it's not polite to slow down time without giving any warning."

"Go ahead, but he didn't know the difference, other than you were in his office one minute and gone the next."

"Then it might be best to leave it at that unless he brings it up."

"Smart." They headed down the hallway to Logan's office. Conveniently, both Logan and Stone were inside. "Hey."

They both looked up. Logan smiled. "I'm glad Danita came to no harm."

Griffin faced Danita. "You want to tell them?"

"You go ahead."

For the next few minutes, he told them how he'd followed Danita to the mine, saw her disappear behind the mine wall, and then followed her back to the condo.

"You followed me?" she asked.

Shit. "I'm sorry. In all of the confusion, I forgot to tell you."

"We'll discuss this later," she said, acting a lot more in control than she ever had before.

Stone placed his fingers in a time out configuration. "You actually found the mine?"

"Yes."

"Where the hell was it?"

That was troublesome. "With your excellent hearing, you should have heard some underground movement. The entrance faced the large field where we landed. It was right behind where Kenton exploded the flash bomb."

They both shook their heads. "We went out there and saw nothing."

"I went inside," Danita said.

"You saw workers and everything?" Stone asked.

"Yes." She described how it was really dark in there, but when she walked to a ledge, she could look down. "There was an elevator that I assumed was to carry the workers to and from the mine."

Logan pushed back his chair. "We need to go again. Can you find it, Griff?"

"Yes, but we need a plan, which means we have to call a meeting."

"I'm on it," Stone said.

Griffin worried about Stone's enthusiasm. He loved a good fight, but he also had a tendency to be hot-headed.

Stone jogged out of the office, presumably to make the necessary calls. The one talent he wished the Guardians had was that of telepathy. If only they had a system where they could silently interact with each other, it would make it so much easier.

"How are you going to get into the cave?" Danita asked. "The opening will only fit someone who is small. Would you like me to go in?"

"No! I'll ask Tory, Kaleena's sister. She is a fierce fighter and small like you."

"Then what can I do? I need to be there for Wendy."

Griffin loved her enthusiasm and desire to help, but she would be no use if a guard grabbed her. "I can't be distracted. The best thing you can do is stay in the condo."

"I need to be there."

He sure as hell wasn't going to fly her there. Yes, she could drive, but that would take a few hours. "We are Guardians, remember?"

"I remember quite well."

"We are also trained fighters. Believe me when I say Wendy has a better chance of being found if you stay safe."

She stuck her tongue out at him. "Fine, but you better find her."

Griffin gathered her in his arms and held her tight. "I will do everything in my power to make sure she is rescued."

"You better."

He kissed the top of her head. "I would like you to be at the meeting of the minds though. You might be able to give us some good intel."

Her smile said it all. "I would love that."

Griffin had asked for her input before when they were hunting Sanditra. This time, she would be there in a better frame of mind.

Stone returned. "All set. I spoke with Declan and Finn. Declan can't make it. Chelsea is having some issue with the pregnancy, but he said he would call the others. Meeting will be in one hour."

"That works." He turned to Danita. "Want to grab something to eat while we wait?"

"Yes. I'm starving."

GRIFFIN STOOD AT the end of the long conference table, facing Thane, Finn, Birk, Stone, Tory, Logan, and Camden. Greer was tending the store, Nessa was out of town with Kyle, and Ramsey said there was a large backlog in the lab and couldn't get away. It wasn't a big deal. If eight Guardians couldn't take down some mining security, they didn't deserve to be Guardians.

"Here is what I'm thinking," Griffin said. "I'd like us to come in piecemeal. Tory and I will head in first."

"Why Tory?" Thane asked. "No offense, sis."

She smiled. "No offense taken." She then gave him the finger in jest.

"Danita, why don't you explain."

"The entrance to the mine is almost completely covered by a

very large stone, but there was a slit just large enough for me to squeeze through."

"None of us are tiny men," Griffin said. "Suffice it to say, Tory is the only person who can pull off this job."

"Thank you, Griffin," his cousin said with a rather smug smile.

"My pleasure. Anyway, Danita did you find any mechanism that would open the large rock that was blocking the entrance? You said there is an elevator inside the door to the right, which would imply there must be an entrance."

She shook her head. "I'm sorry. I was so focused on finding Wendy that it didn't occur to me to look around. As I mentioned before, it was really dark in there. The only lights came from the mine below."

"While my eyesight is excellent," Tory said, "I'll bring a red lamp to search the area. I'm hoping no one will notice it. I'll open the door from the inside if I can."

"Good," Griffin said. "Once that happens, I imagine alarms will sound. I'd like Finn, Thane, Birk, and Camden to be circling above, ready to fight."

"Where would you like me and Stone?" Logan asked.

"As strong back up. We can handle two shifters at a time, assuming their guards are even dragon shifters. If any of us needs help, that's where you come in."

"Got it."

"Tory, as soon as you open the door, I'd like you to survey the area around the mountain for any other possible entrances. I doubt this is the only one. It's possible that if, and that's a big if, the person who kidnapped Wendy is in there, he might try to leave via an alternate exit. We need to be prepared for anything."

"Can do."

Tory was a smart fighter. She had patience where some of the others did not. Griffin went over the plan one more time, making sure everyone was on the same page.

"We've got this," Thane said.

Griffin turned to Danita. "You have to promise me that you will return to the condo. As you can tell, we have everything under control. If we are successful, I will call you. I know there is cell service there because you received a call while there."

"There is, and I promise I will do as you ask. Now that my darkness is gone, I don't have the urge to disobey."

He smiled. "Remind me to find the perfect present for Kenton."

"Who's Kenton?" Tory asked.

"The Fey who was able to remove the piece of dark Fey soul from Danita. He's Fay Forrester's brother."

Birk's eyes widened. "You saw Fay?"

"Yes. I'll catch you up right after we save those held prisoner in the mine."

They pushed back their chairs, ready to go. Griffin hugged Danita. They'd driven from the mine to the SinCas building so that Danita would have a quick way home.

"Be safe," she said.

He kissed her. "Always."

As soon as she stepped into the elevator, he rushed up the stairs to the rooftop, ready to find this mine and save the slaves.

Instead of flying en masse anywhere close to the current Malpan mine, they separated and avoided the area. Even though he only had the word of a criminal that Malpan was behind this, Griffin wanted her to be safe too, in case Malpan was involved.

As they neared the limestone mountains, they all cloaked themselves. Because several of the Guardians had been snooping around before, Griffin assumed there would be sentries waiting for them to return.

It didn't take long for him to spot an opening to the west of the area where Danita had entered the mine. He dove toward the space and Tory followed. Logan and Stone would soon follow while the rest would remain above.

Once he and Tory were on the ground, they both shifted. Moving through the forested area was a lot faster in their human form.

They were experts at concealing themselves, using the trees and rocks as their camouflage. Those skills were taught as soon as they learned to shift. Dodging from one tree to the next was something that was now ingrained in all of them.

Like the well-practiced team they were, Griffin and Tory made their way from tree to tree. Even though they were a few hundred feet from the mine entrance, Griffin searched for any trip wires but found none.

At the edge of the field, he motioned for Tory to halt. After waiting a few minutes without any visits from sentries, they dashed across the field, keeping to the edge, hoping to avoid any surveillance. Thane, who was above, would screech if he noticed an army of sentries anywhere on the property.

So far so good.

In case there were motion sensors, they kept low and made their way to the large rock. Tory's goal was to enter and look for a latch or button that would open the large rock from the inside. She slipped on her red headlamp and activated it. With a quick smile, she wedged her way through the small opening and disappeared. Griffin plastered his back against the hillside, constantly searching for security. What struck him as odd was the lack of activity underneath them. He edged sideways toward the opening and peeked in. This time, no sounds were coming from the entrance either.

His scales hardened, readying him for something to come. The rock behind him moved, and he stepped out of the way. The mechanism to open the rock was not silent. Shit. The miners would have to know they weren't alone now.

"Hurry," he whispered.

Once the door opened wide enough, Tory rushed out. "I looked over the balcony structure. I could see a lot of mining equipment but no workers."

"Fuck. They have to be somewhere. Head out around to the left to see if you can find that other entrance—an entrance that might be hidden. I'll go right." He didn't believe the owner would move the slaves just because some people had landed in the field outside of their mine. Oh, crap. Maybe someone had spotted Danita when she was inside.

Tory gave him a quick smile and then rushed away as quietly as a dragon could fly. Griffin hadn't gone but a few feet when a wave of dark blue dragon shifters came around from the left. There were eight of them. Logan and Stone knew enough to wait until the battle was underway before showing themselves, but hopefully the rest of the Guardians would come swooping in—as in now.

As the blue dragons zeroed in on him, Griffin eyed them, trying to decide which one was their leader. Take him out, and the rest might panic. He must have been too focused on his decision, because it took a few seconds before he was aware of the wave of Guardian power that was near.

Griffin shot upward and flew toward the dragon in front. Several of the blue dragons shrieked. When cloaked, the Guardians were totally invisible. He imagined it would be rather upsetting to suddenly be rammed from on top or attacked from below without any forewarning. Two of the sentries immediately plummeted to the ground, seemingly injured but not dead. One appeared to have a torn wing, but Griffin didn't have the time to assess the other one's injuries.

Two down, six to go. Thane chose to go after two at a time probably because he was the best-trained fighter of the group. That left each of them with only one. Griffin's dragon executed a large loop around him. While he could have cloaked himself, he wanted to save the energy. Besides, he liked the challenge.

Claws extended and fire spewing from his mouth, his adversary charged. Griffin let him move in close, pretending to be paralyzed with fear. At the last second, Griffin ducked and flipped over, enabling him to reach up and claw the dragon's underbelly. While not a fatal blow, it would slow him down. The loud screech confirmed he'd been injured. Killing wasn't Griffin's favorite thing to do, and he wouldn't do that now. These guards were hired help. It was possible, though not probable, that they didn't know what was really going on inside the mine. If that was the case, they were innocent. Griffin's goal was to maim, not destroy. The Guardians just needed time to save the slaves. Then they'd be gone.

Wings flapped, screeches rent through the air, and fireballs were shooting everywhere. Twice he'd had to dodge an errant stream. His attacker flew off and then landed. He wasn't done, but clearly he needed some time to recharge. In the meantime, Griffin would help out Thane. While his cousin seemed to be doing well against two rather talented fighters, it never hurt to lend a hand until Griffin's original sentry returned.

Beating his wings hard, Griffin reached the second dragon shifter who was scratching the crap out of Thane's right wing. Using his nose, Griffin rammed into the animal's side, causing him to let go of his hold. Thane shot a blast of fire into the air as a thank you. Needing to incapacitate this one and fast, he went straight for the heart. Griffin did a maneuver meant to distract, turning the blue sentry around. He was not only better trained than this dragon, Griffin was faster too. Dipping under and a little behind the dragon, his movements caused the beast to twist around. At the last second, Griffin cloaked himself and charged. His claws found their mark. The animal buckled and fluttered. His trip to the ground was quick and hard.

Griffin was about to see if anyone else needed his help, when the first animal who attacked him returned. That was a mistake on the sentry's part. Griffin attacked. This time, his foe's injuries could prove fatal.

Out of the corner of his eye, Griffin spotted three more dragons emerging from the left side of the mine—where Tory was investigating. Damn. As if they knew it was time, Logan and Stone emerged from the forested area. Then Tory shot upward. Good. The Guardians who'd been fighting could handle those who'd arrive first. Stone, Logan, and Tory would have no problem putting down the other dragons.

Chapter Eighteen

"WHY DIDN'T YOU tell Griffin that there is another dark Fey on Tarradon? Or tell me?" Fay asked.

Kenton stabbed a hand through his hair. "Griffin has enough on his plate. I didn't mention it to you because I didn't think it was important at the time. Now I can see I was wrong."

"You do realize what would happen if the Fey finds Danita?"

"Yes. A second dose of that evil might kill her. At best, she'd be turned, never to be saved. Don't worry. I won't let Malpan anywhere near her."

Fay crossed her arms. "Do you know where he is so you can stop him?"

"I just returned from searching for him."

"And?"

"Malpan is at the mine. When I looked into the pool, I saw Griffin and his men heading out there."

Her jaw dropped. "Our job is to protect the Guardians. No telling what Malpan will do once he finds out that Griffin and the others want to destroy his property."

Kenton held up his hand. "I only came back here to let you know. I'm heading there now. Don't worry. I'll stop him."

His sister held out her hand. "What are you waiting for?"

Fay was too bossy sometimes. He had it under control. They were supposed to protect the Guardians—guide them in the right direction, so to speak—not fight their battles for them. Since Malpan was a dark Fey, either Kenton or Bevon had to be the ones to deal with him. How he'd escaped their realm in the first place was anyone's guess, but Kenton would see that the man was returned to his rightful place.

One second Kenton was standing next to his sister at the eternal flame and the next he was in the woods by the mine. Not sensing anyone near, he edged closer to the large field that sat in front of the stone entrance.

A mechanical noise reached him. This came from the far left side of the large mountain. Not wanting to be seen, he teleported to the line of trees in front of where the noise had come from. A beautiful blonde emerged from behind a large stone, and Kenton's heart beat hard. Who was she?

One second she was human, and the next she was soaring upward. Her stunning yellow scales shone brightly against her black ones, making her look like a goddess. Distracted by the lust coursing through him, Kenton almost missed the evil vibrating through him. Damn it. Malpan was near. From the same entrance the blonde woman had emerged came two more people. One was Malpan. The other was a pretty brunette that Malpan was dragging. Her hands were tied behind her back, and she was gagged. The urge to rip out Malpan's heart right then and there was strong, but the man deserved something worse than a quick death. Something far worse.

A battle was waging overhead. In fact, the yellow and black-scaled dragon was fighting a dragon of her own, but Kenton couldn't become distracted.

Malpan and his captive woman were moving toward him. Kenton hid behind a tree, waiting for a chance to engage in a nice little conversation with Malpan before Kenton sent him home to Feyrion. The two entered the forest and then headed down a path that probably led to a hidden vehicle.

Kenton stepped into the open. "Well, well, if it isn't Mr. Malpan. Let go of the woman."

Malpan's eyes widened. A Fey could sense another Fey. He bet Malpan had no idea his Fey family was on Tarradon. Nor would he have any idea how powerful the Foresters were.

"Get out of my way," Malpan said, moving his hostage in front of him. If that was his way of protecting himself, the man was a bigger coward than Kenton could ever have imagined.

"Be a man and let her go. Or are you too much of a coward to face me alone?" Not that there would be a fight. No. Kenton had other ways to dispose of this creep.

"You don't understand."

This ought to be good. "Is that so? Then tell me."

"You can never know how hard my life has been since my son died."

That did tug on Kenton's heartstrings. Family was everything to him. "What happened to him?"

"My son was working at the Caspian mines when there was an accident—one that *they* could have prevented."

Not that Kenton spoke with a lot of people who lived in Edendale, but he doubted any Guardian would run anything but a top-notch business. "He was killed?"

"No, he was run over by a rail car, which caused him to lose his leg. My son became so despondent that he killed himself."

"You could have asked for our help." Or had Malpan been denied entry back into their Fey realm because of his darkness?

"I didn't know there were other Feys here—at least none at the time."

"I meant Feys in Feyrion."

"My mate is from Tarradon. I didn't want to leave her."

That sounded so lame. "Go on."

"When my son died, my wife left me, and I turned bitter. Oh, so bitter."

"Is that why you enslaved all of these men?" Kenton asked. "To get back at the Caspians?"

"Yes. I wanted to ruin them like they did me. With free labor, I can charge lower prices and drive them out of business."

"That is truly despicable behavior."

Malpan lifted his chin. "To you, maybe."

"No. To all decent beings. The Caspians are a large family. I bet it would be extremely hard to do much damage to their bottom line."

"It was a lot easier than I thought. I hired someone to put a spell on the men so they would want to work for me—for free. The men I found were homeless or out of work anyway. I provided them with food and shelter. I did them a service."

Kenton laughed. "You mean Balkin put a spell on them to turn them into mindless slaves?"

Malpan's face paled. "You know Balkin?"

"Let's just say that particular dark Fey is now where he belongs—in our realm—but why not do the spells yourself? You're certainly capable."

"The less connection I had with this mine, the less chance I'd have of being connected to it." He jerked Wendy's arm. "Until this one came along asking all sorts of questions."

Malpan's hand shook so much that Wendy was able to wrench her body out of his grasp. She half ran, half stumbled toward Kenton who moved her behind him. Kenton might have taken the time to undo her bindings, but he didn't want anything to take away from what he needed to do next.

"Condran and Hinton," he telepathed. *"I will be sending a dark Fey through the portal in a moment. Be prepared to accept him."*

"Yes, sir," came the quick response.

Perfect. "Let me ask you this," Kenton said. "After your son was injured, did you go to the Caspians and ask them to get your son help?"

"No. I went to Sanditra instead. She lent me some of her dark Fey magic and made me the man I am today."

That was one stubborn father. He must not have really cared for his son after all. "Why not at least talk to the Caspians? They might have paid for your sons medical bills and gotten him therapy." In truth, Kenton had no idea what they had done to compensate for his son's injury.

"I didn't want them to know he was my son," Malpan mumbled.

The dilemma suddenly became clear. "Don't tell me you sent your son in there to steal their mining operation ideas?"

"Fuck you."

Just then another wave of lust shot through Kenton. He glanced at the sky for a moment, spotting the female dragon with the yellow scales fighting not one, but two blue dragons. She screeched and then fell, tumbling through the trees' canopy of leaves and branches, her wings ripping before she landed on the ground with a thud. More than anything, Kenton wanted to help her, but before he could, she groaned and shifted.

She must be okay then. Using what looked like a great deal of effort, the woman rose to her feet. Just then, Malpan rushed over, grabbed her, and screamed, "I'm not going back to Feyrion."

Like hell he wasn't. "Yes, you are. Get away from the woman."

With a wave of one hand, Kenton caused a huge blast of wind that separated the woman from Malpan's grasp. Then using both hands, he created a portal. He tossed Malpan backward using his telekinetic abilities. One second Malpan was on Tarradon, and the next he was on his way to where he belonged. The portal closed.

Behind him, the brunette dropped to her knees, tears streaming down her cheeks. She mumbled something, and Kenton immediately lowered her gag. She coughed. "Where did he go?"

Shit. Kenton probably should have put a spell on her so that she didn't have to see that, but the wave of desire was still coursing through him so hard, it had blocked his ability to think clearly. "To a place where he will never return from."

Kenton untied her wrists and then rushed over to the blonde who was just standing there in a daze, weaving.

"Are you okay?" he asked her. Kenton wanted to hold her and comfort her, until he suddenly became aware of an evil that was slowly building inside her. Oh, no!

Before the woman could answer, she collapsed.

No! No! No! As Malpan's last departing move, he must have

infected her, just like Sanditra had done to Danita. Yes, this lovely blonde had fallen a good distance, but even on the ground, she didn't appear to have any severe injuries.

Crap. Why did the bad ones have to insist on leaving a piece of themselves in someone else? At least once Malpan reached Feyrion, his soul would be removed and destroyed.

Kenton dropped to his knees. For the first time in his life, he wasn't sure what to do. She should have stayed in her dragon form in order to heal, but with a piece of Malpan's dark soul inside her now, she might not be able to shift back to her animal.

"Bevon, I need your help," he telepathed to his brother. A Fey was this woman's best chance of saving her.

"Where are you?" came the reply.

"By the limestone mine I was telling you about."

"What's wrong?"

Jeez. For once, couldn't he do what he was asked without questioning it? *"Just get here now."*

As he waited for his brother, the squawking and screeching sounds overhead stopped.

"Tory?" came a shot from the woods. It was Griffin. Good, he might know what to do.

THE FIGHT LASTED longer than Griffin would have wished, but he was happy he was able to account for all of the Guardians except for Tory. Where the hell was she? It was possible she was catching her breath after being hurt.

Finn looked the least affected by the fight. While he was new to the Guardians, his skills when learning to fight as a wolf shifter made the transition to a dragon fighter easier. Not only that, newcomers were always very strong at first.

"Anyone see Tory?" Griffin asked.

Stone shifted into his human form and came toward him. His

legs and torso were a bit bloodied, but he would heal quickly once he gave his dragon more time to help with that. "I saw her fall near the north corner. There's an entrance over there. It's where those other dragons came from."

"I'll check on her. Go see if you can find the prisoners and then help them, but be careful. There might be armed guards inside—ones who were smart enough not to engage with us in our shifter form."

"The six of us can handle anything they dish out."

Griffin glanced around the grounds. All of the blue dragons had either flown off, were mortally wounded, or were slow to recover. "One of you needs to stay outside and make sure these dragons leave."

Stone saluted. "Can do."

With the mine secure, he went in search of his cousin. "Tory?" he called.

A muffled sound reached him, but it didn't sound like a female's voice. Cautious, Griffin moved in the direction of the call. Through the trees, he spotted what looked like a man on his knees, hovering over a blonde woman. Oh, shit.

Griffin ditched his caution and ran down the path, stopping abruptly when he spotted another woman sitting on the ground, dirty and scared. It was Kenton who was leaning over Tory.

While he had healed Danita, he wasn't sure if Kenton had any abilities when it came to physical injuries. Griffin scanned Tory's body, but he only detected a few scratches. He knelt on the other side of her. "Tory? It's me, Griffin. Open your eyes."

She didn't move.

He waited for Kenton to add his opinion, but he said nothing as he kept his hands on her shoulders. It was almost as if he was running some kind of Fey diagnostics. Kenton rocked back on his heels and looked at Griffin. "She is dying."

Griffin nearly collapsed. "That's not possible. She barely has a scratch on her. I'll fly her to Declan. He can save her."

"No, he can't. She's been infected with Fey dark magic—Malpan's dark magic to be exact. It is preventing her dragon from healing her."

Kenton wasn't making any sense. "Malpan did this?" Griffin looked around. "How? Where is he?"

"I sent him back to our Fey realm." Kenton nodded to the brunette on her knees. "Malpan was the one who captured this woman."

That was unacceptable. "He needs to return here and pay for his crimes."

Kenton placed a hand on Griffin's shoulder. "I did what I had to do. Trust me, the punishment on our realm will be much worse than anything you could do to him here."

Griffin hoped that was true. The other woman rubbed her wrists and moaned. While Griffin had seen a picture of Wendy before, this woman certainly didn't look anything like that. "Are you Wendy by any chance?"

"I am."

Griffin rose and moved over to her. "Tell me what happened."

"Malpan broke into my apartment and kidnapped me. I had learned some missing men might have been kidnapped and were being used as slaves. As a journalist, I wanted to write a story about it, but Malpan found out somehow and came after me."

While Griffin wanted to learn about all of the details, he needed to get help for Tory first.

Leaves rustled and from behind a tree stepped another man who looked remarkably liked Kenton. Kenton looked up. "This is my brother Bevon. He's come to help me with…Tory."

"Is your brother a doctor?" Between Greer and Declan, Griffin was certain they could heal her.

"No, but we are Feys. As I told you, Malpan was a dark Fey. When Tory crashed through the trees to the ground, she was stunned. For some reason she shifted into her human form. That was when Malpan grabbed her, but then he realized I was from Feyrion. He must have realized I could send him back there to where his soul would be lost forever, so he infected Tory."

"What *exactly* will happen to Malpan now that he's on Feyrion?"

"His dark soul will be ripped from his body, and his darkness will be put in a safe place, right next to Sanditra's dark soul."

Griffin dropped to the ground. "I can't believe she has the same evil inside her as Danita had."

"Yes."

"You two can't take it out of her? You did for Danita."

"Not here we can't. This is different because a part of Malpan's soul seems to have gone straight into Tory's dragon. While Bevon and I are quite powerful, we will need even more magic—the kind that is only found in our realm."

"You want to take Tory to your realm?" Griffin couldn't let that happen.

"Don't worry. Once she is free of this evil, we will return."

The Guardians could create a portal between Tarradon and Earth, but he had no idea how to make one to this Fey realm. "How do I know you'll come back?"

"I give you my word," Kenton said.

Of all the Guardians, Griffin was the level headed one. But ever since Danita had walked into his life, his world had been turned upside down. His ability to think logically and without much emotion had been compromised, though the Four Sisters had vouched for these men. "I'd like to speak with her family about this. It's a big decision."

Kenton glanced up at Bevon.

Bevon shook his head. "She doesn't have the time."

"How do you know? You barely examined her."

Kenton held up his hand. "Bevon has talents. Detecting evil in others is one of them."

"You're telling me that she will die unless you leave now?"

"Yes," Bevon said.

This was out of Griffin's scope. "How long will it take to rid her of this evil soul?"

VELLA DAY

Bevon blew out a breath. "It's hard to say."

As if she wanted to stay, Tory's arm moved and then her back arched up. When she didn't open her eyes, concern welled inside of him. What was happening? "Tory, can you hear me?" Griffin asked.

"She's going into dark shock. The darkness is too much for her body to handle, and her dragon is rebelling. We have to leave now," Kenton said, sounding close to panicking.

He scooped Tory into his arms while Bevon created a portal. Griffin wanted to do what was best for her. Having her leave this realm scared the shit out of him though. "Go, but you better return."

"I promise."

A second later, all three disappeared. Griffin slumped down. Oh, my goddess. What had he done?

Chapter Nineteen

W HEN DANITA'S PHONE rang, she stopped pacing. It was Griffin. "Are you okay?" she asked, her voice shaking.

"Yes, and so is Wendy."

Danita's knees almost buckled. The news was too good to be true. "I can't believe you found her." Saying Wendy was okay didn't tell her all that much though. Danita needed the details. What was her cousin's state of mind? Her health status?

"We did. I'll tell you all about it when we return."

"Where are you?"

His inhale sounded more like exasperation than taking a deep breath. "We're at the mine. Wendy is going to help us to find all of the prisoners before we head back. Malpan was behind all of this. I promise I'll tell you all about it when I see you."

"When will that be?" There was something in his voice that sounded more strained than usual.

"Soon. Don't worry. I'll be home when I can. I want to make sure the slaves are taken care of. Hold on a sec."

Shouts and some commotion sounded in the background. She should probably let him do his job. As long as he and Wendy were okay, she could deal with waiting for as long as need be.

"That was Bevon returning from his Fey world."

"Bevon? I thought his name was Kenton."

"Another long story. Listen, I gotta go."

"Sure thing." She disconnected, a bit upset that he hadn't been able to talk.

Danita dropped down onto the barstool, anxious to be reunited with her cousin again. She couldn't believe that Griffin and the Guardians had found Wendy. The fact her cousin was healthy enough to help them locate the prisoners thrilled her to no end.

Danita stilled. While Wendy might be physically fine, Danita understood all too well what it was like to be held prisoner against her will, and what it could do to a person's psyche.

Before she drove herself crazy thinking about what was really going through Wendy's mind, Danita fixed herself a cup of hot chocolate. And then another. When Griffin still hadn't returned home, she picked up a book from his coffee table and looked through it—a coffee table book of Thedia Province. She had to admit the mountains and forests looked lovely, but they didn't truly hold her attention.

Two hours later, the door finally opened. Danita set down the book and jumped up. Her heart raced. She didn't know who to hug first—her cousin who was rather disheveled and dirty, but who had a smile on her face, or her mate who looked like he'd lost the battle.

Wendy took the option out of her hands when she flung herself into Danita's arms. "Thank you for saving me."

Danita leaned back. "I didn't do anything. I was here the whole time."

"Griffin told me you had some kind of vision that led them to the mine in the first place."

"I did, but Griffin and his group freed you."

"Actually, Kenton saved me," Wendy said. "Don't get me wrong. Griffin and his men were heroes too. They were able to take out the security, which allowed them to free the slaves."

Danita was a bit confused about Kenton's role in all of this, but she could wait to learn more later. "I am so happy that everything turned out so well. Griffin is a hero. Oh, where are my manners. Can I get you something to drink or eat? You must be starving." Her cousin looked as if she'd lost weight.

Wendy smiled. "I am really hungry, but what I need even more is to head on home and take a shower. I can't stand this filth any longer."

Griffin placed a hand on her shoulder. "Please stay here—at least for the night. You shouldn't be alone, especially after what you've been through. We have plenty of room."

Her mate was the nicest person in the world.

Wendy smiled. "I'd like that, but what about these?" She plucked her shirt off her body.

"Don't worry. I'll lend you some fresh clothes. We're about the same size. I'll show you where you can shower."

Wendy hugged Danita again. "You are the best."

As soon as her cousin was settled, Danita returned to the living room. Griffin was facing the front window with a beer in his hand, staring off into the darkness of the night sky. She moved in front of him, waiting for him to notice she was even there. When he didn't respond, she tapped his arm. "Hey, where did you go?"

He looked down at her and briefly smiled. "Just going over the events of the day."

"You're not acting yourself. Was someone hurt?"

"Let's sit down."

A giant claw grabbed her stomach. "Tell me."

"I don't know the full story since I wasn't there at the time, but according to Kenton, Malpan got a hold of Tory and infected her with his dark soul—the same kind of darkness that came from Sanditra."

She grabbed Griffin's hand. "Oh, no. Are you saying that Malpan was a dark Fey like Sanditra?"

"Yes."

Her mind raced at the horror. "Was Kenton able to help her like he did me?"

Griffin shook his head. "He said Malpan's soul infected Tory's dragon. She can't shift nor can her dragon heal her. She never regained consciousness." His jaw clenched, and his breathing increased.

"That's terrible. What did you do?" Danita worked to keep her voice steady.

Griffin turned to her. "In order to save Tory, I allowed Kenton to take her to his realm. He promised he could heal her there."

He wasn't making any sense. "What do you mean? To his realm?" Then she vaguely remembered Kenton saying something about taking Sanditra's soul to his realm.

Griffin detailed the entire conversation. "Bevon, who is Kenton's brother, made a portal, and the three of them just disappeared with Tory, who was out cold at the time."

"She was unconscious before Malpan did this to her?"

"No. Apparently, Tory had been in battle and fell to the ground. A few seconds later, she rose under her own power. Malpan moved close to her, and the next second she collapsed. Neither Bevon nor Kenton could rouse her. She didn't even respond to my voice. It was as if Malpan had frozen her mind."

He was speaking metaphorically of course. Even still, something wasn't adding up. "If Kenton and Bevon carried Tory into this other realm, how could Bevon be at the mine when you called me? This isn't making any sense."

"Bevon came back. He said that Tory was in good hands, and that she would return eventually."

"Eventually?"

Griffin looked straight ahead and then grunted. "I need to go." He stood.

"Go? Where? You just got here." He was hurting, and she wanted to help him.

"I have to tell Jamison and Moira what happened. I owe them an explanation for why their daughter will not be returning home."

"You mean she won't be returning right away."

"Yes." He leaned over and kissed her quickly. "Fix something to eat for your cousin. I'm sure you have a lot to catch up on."

"We do."

As much as she didn't want Griffin to leave, he seemed highly upset and in need of some solitude. She could only hope that Tory's parents wouldn't blame him for what happened. Griffin wasn't the one who'd infected her with darkness—Malpan had.

Too bad Griffin didn't seem to understand that by letting his cousin go with Kenton, he might have saved her life—not ruined it.

Once he left, Danita just stood there trying to digest what had happened. The shower water turned off in the guest bedroom. Oh, crap. Danita had promised Wendy something to eat. She rushed over to the kitchen and pulled a chicken casserole out of the refrigerator. A small smile lifted her lips for a split second. Wendy had given her this recipe. Being hungry herself, Danita warmed up two servings.

Her cousin walked out of the spare bedroom wearing one of Danita's T-shirts and a pair of stretch jeans. "They look good on you," Danita said, trying to sound cheerful.

Wendy laughed. "I think they are about three inches too short, but I am incredibly thankful for clean clothes." She held up her wrists. "Do you have any ointment for these? Malpan kept my wrists tied the whole time."

"I am so sorry this happened to you." Danita understood how uncomfortable cuffs could be. She walked over to her cousin and examined the red marks. While they looked painful, they didn't appear to be infected. "Let me see what we have. Because Griffin is a dragon shifter, he might not have much. I only moved in a while ago and thankfully haven't needed any first aid supplies."

"It's okay if you don't have anything. I'll live."

Brave Wendy. "I'll check. Go ahead and grab something to drink while I look."

To her delight, when Danita searched the bathroom cabinet under the sink, she found a first aid kit. Upon inspection, she noticed it had never been used. No time like the present to break it open.

Danita carried it out to her cousin. "You're in luck."

"Awesome." Wendy took it from her and opened the case. "Are you sure it's okay to break the seal?"

Danita smiled. "I'm sure."

Once Wendy put ointment on her wrists and Danita helped bandage them, she pulled the heated food from the oven and placed it on the table. They then sat down to dinner.

"Where did Griffin go?" Wendy asked.

"He wanted to speak to Tory's parents about what happened."

She exhaled and shook her head. "I can't imagine having to make that decision, but from the way she wasn't moving, she might have died if Kenton hadn't taken her to wherever he took her."

Griffin had explained about the portal, but Danita wanted to be sure she understood. "Kenton just picked Tory up and then walked her through some kind of force field?"

"Yup, along with his brother."

"Griffin said the brother returned shortly thereafter. That bodes well for Tory, I guess."

"I hope so," Wendy said.

Only then did Danita realize she hadn't shared any personal information with her cousin in over a week, so she couldn't know that Kenton had been able to remove the dark Fey magic from Danita's soul. "I have faith that she will and here's why." She told her about her trip to the eternal flame.

Wendy's eyes brightened. "You no longer have any darkness in you?"

"Nope."

"I am so happy for you."

Danita smiled. "Me too. Now tell me about you, unless the whole experience is still too raw." Danita hadn't been willing to speak of her ordeal after she was first released. "Malpan didn't infect you, did he?"

"No. I think he only wanted to use me as a bargaining chip. He told me that I was asking too many questions, and he needed to stop me, but I don't think that's the whole reason he had his goons kidnap me. I heard Malpan's confession and learned why he did everything."

"Griffin didn't mention anything about a confession."

Wendy lifted a shoulder. "I told him what Malpan said, but I think he was still too upset about Tory to really pay attention." Her cousin told her about Malpan's reasoning for enslaving the men, and it mostly made sense.

"All this was for revenge?" Danita asked. "The slaves and your capture?"

"Apparently."

"I'm still confused why he would take you. Sure, he didn't want you finding out about his slave ring, but why not just kill you? You have no connection to the Caspians, other than through me."

"Through you?"

Heat raced up Danita's face. She couldn't believe how much had transpired since Wendy had been taken. "Ah, Griffin told me we were mates."

Wendy grinned. "That is amazing. Your life has literally turned around while I was gone."

"I know. I thought about you so much. I'm still a little in shock about what has happened, but the fact I am living here should have clued you in that we are together."

"Together, together?" Wendy's eyes sparkled.

"Yes." While it might not be nice to have such joy in her voice, Danita couldn't help it. Wendy had been searching for her mate for what seemed like forever.

"That is fantastic. And yes, I should have figured it out when I found you at Griffin's place. I figured maybe you were in danger, and he wanted to keep you safe."

It was a reasonable assumption since Griffin had been her protector ever since she'd been freed from the castle prison. "That might have been the initial plan, but then things kind of worked themselves out."

Wendy laughed. "I am thrilled for you. Truly. I should have realized it earlier, but I'm still a little preoccupied with what went down."

"Of course. Tell me what happened." Danita took a bite of the casserole, which tasted better than when she'd first made it.

Wendy detailed how two goons had come to her door. "They knocked. Being careful, I looked through the peephole, but since they were dressed in suits, I answered. My mistake. They barged in and grabbed me."

"You didn't shift?" Wendy claimed she was quite a good fighter and had even taken some self-defense classes.

"I did shift, but before I could inflict any damage, I felt something sting my neck, and when I woke up, I was in a locked room. I wasn't sure where I was until I was freed from that terrible mine. The smell, the dampness, and the lack of natural light will take a long time to forget."

Danita reached across the table and clasped her hand. "I am so sorry."

"Thanks. I think the hardest part was trying to figure out why someone would go to that much trouble to take me. I didn't have any proof that Malpan was involved in trafficking. I just had a hunch."

"You must have been so scared," Danita said.

"I was. The first few days I was upbeat thinking these people would realize they had the wrong person. Then I began to give up hope."

"I hear you. I totally gave up hope when I was in that prison, but you had to know I'd be looking for you."

Wendy picked up her glass and sipped her drink, probably trying to think of whether or not to express her true feelings. "I did think you'd try to find me, but come on, Danita. You were struggling so much with your own demons that I figured you had enough to deal with. Besides, what could you really have done?" She waved her fork. "Even when he made me call you, I thought it was to capture you not help save me."

"That thought crossed my mind, but I figured I could slow down time and run off with you." She explained how she was able to do that now.

"I would have liked to have seen that."

Danita smiled. "I try to only do it if it is for good."

"I get it."

"Did Malpan ever mention my name specifically?" Danita asked.

"Not until he came in and said it was time to call you."

"He somehow must have known of my connection with Griffin."

"Yes. I imagine the miners run in a small circle. Malpan probably knew someone who told him that Griffin really cared for you," Wendy said.

All this talk was bringing her down again, and she just needed to be thankful all was well—or rather almost well.

The door clicked, her heart jumped, and then Griffin came in. While she couldn't read his mind, it was clear he was upset.

Danita pushed back from the table. "How did it go?" she asked as she rushed up to him.

"They were understanding."

That sounded good. "But?"

"I can't help but think I should have done more for Tory."

Why did Griffin always seem to carry the weight of the world on his shoulders? "Like what? You aren't a healer. Even if you'd flown back to Edendale and asked Declan or Greer to join you, neither healer could have gotten there fast enough to save her."

"That's what phones are for."

"Seriously? It still would have taken some time for them to fly there and find you. When they did, they couldn't have removed a Fey's dark soul. Remember, even the Four Sisters couldn't do it, so why would you think Declan or Greer could?"

"You're right. They couldn't have. I definitely wasn't thinking clearly at the time. Seeing Tory so still like that totally unnerved me."

Wendy pushed back her chair from the dining room table, stood, and came over to them. "You did what Tory needed. You heard what that man said. Tory didn't have much time left. He confirmed that neither Greer nor Declan would have been able to remove the piece of Malpan from Tory's dragon."

"She's right," Danita said. "That was why Poppy sent us to him."

He nodded. "I know it was the right decision, but if I had insisted that three or four of us make up the first landing party instead of just Tory and me, she would have had more help. What were the odds that she would fall right where Malpan was standing?"

Griffin's pain reached her. He seemed to be looking for reasons to blame himself. "If you think that way, why not blame me for having the premonition that led you to the mountains in the first place?"

"Or me for snooping too much into Malpan's affairs?" Wendy asked.

"Fine. You two ladies win," he said, though he didn't sound all that convincing.

Danita rubbed his arm. "When Kenton returns with Tory, she'll thank you for getting her help so soon."

He blew out a breath. "Logically, I know that to be true, but emotionally, it's difficult to accept." He leaned over and kissed Danita lightly. "I need to take a shower."

"Don't you want something to eat first? I can heat you up some chicken casserole."

"No, thank you."

Okay, that was so not good.

Chapter Twenty

ONCE WENDY HEADED to bed, Danita cleaned up the kitchen. Griffin had finished showering about twenty minutes ago, and she expected him to return to the living room. Apparently, she'd been wrong. She could only hope he was waiting for her to go to him. Being the considerate man he was, he probably figured that she and Wendy needed to spend time together. After all, her cousin had just survived a rather traumatic experience, and he probably thought Danita would want to be there for her.

After turning off the lights, Danita pushed open the bedroom door to find it was dark inside.

"Griffin?" she whispered.

"I'm not asleep."

"You're in bed early." He claimed dragon shifters didn't need a lot of sleep.

"I thought you and Wendy would want to talk. Besides, I'm not good company right now."

The anguish in his tone nearly cut her. She slipped off her clothes and slid into bed, hoping to bring him out of his funk. Of all people, she understood what depression and self-loathing could do to a person. "Talk to me."

"It's not something you need to worry about."

That pissed her off. "Are we fated for each other or not?"

He stiffened and then rolled onto his side to face her. "Of course we are!"

"If that's true, I want to help you. Sometimes just talking to someone else about whatever is bothering you can help clear your head." She suspected he was still feeling guilty about Tory.

He stroked her face, leaned over, and kissed her lightly. "Thank you, but there is nothing to discuss."

"Griffin Caspian."

"Fine. If you must know, I'm second-guessing myself about letting some guy I just met take my cousin to another freaking realm. Who does that?"

"You did what you thought was best for her."

He rolled onto his back and crossed his arms over his naked chest. "Did I?"

Danita unfolded his arms and placed her cheek on his chest. While she might not be able to absorb his pain, she wanted to lessen it. "Yes, you did, and I promise that when she comes back, she'll thank you."

"Assuming she returns at all."

She'd had enough of this self-loathing. Danita sat up, twisted around, and faced him. "Don't do this to yourself."

He rubbed her leg. Even though Griffin wasn't taking out his anger on her, it still hurt to see him this way.

"You're a white lighter, not a Fey or a Fairy. What do you know about this Kenton guy?"

"I know that he healed me. That makes him a hero in my mind." Griffin winced. Shit. "I just meant that he's never done anything to show that he is anything but good. You even said, his sister helped Nessa and Birk."

"I did."

"Poppy vouched for him to help me, and you think the world of the Four Sisters."

"True."

Ugh. She wasn't getting through to him. "How about we snuggle, and you try to clear your mind of all the guilt you are feeling—at least for the night?"

He looked over at her and smiled briefly. "You are an amazing woman."

"If I were truly amazing, you'd be inside of me right now."

Griffin turned his head. "I'm sorry, but when I make love to you, I want to give you my full attention."

He was sweet, and even though she wanted to strangle him, he didn't need the added pressure. Danita crawled in next to him, and wrapped her arms around his waist. She held her breath waiting to see what Griffin would do. A moment later, he pulled her closer.

"Thank you," he said.

She looked up at him. "For what?"

"For being there for me."

A moment later, soft snores filled the room. Danita sagged against him, content that maybe she'd helped give him a little peace.

GRIFFIN JOLTED AWAKE from his not-so-pleasant dream. Soft light from the early dawn was filtering in through the window. Snuggled against him was Danita. It seemed as if she'd just come into the bedroom to talk to him, and yet here it was morning already.

More guilt swamped him. She had been trying to help, and what had he done? He'd fallen asleep on her. What was wrong with him? She'd practically begged that they make love, and he basically told her he wasn't fit company for it. He was a jerk. At the very least, he should thank her for calming his mind enough to let him get some sleep.

Griffin would have to make it up to her later—after he accomplished his one goal, which was to learn all he could about the Forrester family. Bevon had entered that Feyrion realm and returned shortly thereafter. Surely, he'd be willing to go back and check on his brother and Tory. If this family was so upstanding, he'd do that, right?

As much as Griffin wanted to wake up his sleeping beauty and kiss her silly, Danita had been through a lot lately, especially with her having to wait for him for so many hours last night. While he did bring back her cousin, he'd left immediately. Knowing Danita, his actions had stressed her out something fierce. He had to hand it to her though. She'd appeared calm.

With great care, he slipped out of her grasp, making sure not to wake her. After he cleaned up and dressed, he stepped into the kitchen, thankful Wendy's door was still closed. Not wanting Danita to worry when she awoke to find him gone, he jotted down a note telling her he wanted to visit Bevon Forrester. She'd understand why.

Once he placed the note on the kitchen counter, he left and headed straight to the rooftop.

The flight to the center of the realm gave him time to think. Griffin was highly thankful that Malpan was no longer in this realm, because it ensured that Wendy and Danita would be safe. Wendy said that Kenton mentioned someone by the name of Balkin who had infected the slaves, turning them basically into zombies. She honestly couldn't remember much more about the conversation between Kenton and Malpan though. Griffin was just happy she remembered as much as she had. He had to hand it to her. Anyone who had been held captive in a dark, cold mine for an extended time was special, especially if they could focus on anything other than being grateful they'd been found. That said a lot about her.

When Griffin spotted the edge of the forest, he landed. After shifting, he jogged down the path, anxious to find one of the Forresters. They should be able to give him an update on Tory's condition or be able to return to their realm and ask him.

Once Griffin arrived at the flame, there were two families there, both with small children. Crap. It didn't surprise him that none of the Feys or Fairies were there as tour guides.

To bide his time until they left, he decided to find the cabin where he and Danita had spent the night, and where Kenton had removed her dark magic. He hoped the cabin would give him a clue as to the location of this Feyrion realm. Kenton had mentioned something about the cabin being a portal to there. Griffin highly doubted there would be an arrow pointing to a big red button that read: push here to enter the Feyrion realm. Instead, he had the sense that just by entering the cabin, he would be transported there.

Griffin remembered Kenton walking down the hallway and exiting out the back. What confused him was that he didn't remember seeing a door back there. Griffin kicked himself for not checking out the place more thoroughly that first time he had been inside. Then again, he'd just made love to Danita, and his hormones were swirling inside him.

As Griffin headed down the trail, he kept his eyes peeled. The first time he came down this path, he remembered walking about a half-mile before reaching the cabin. So what if the damn thing seemed to have disappeared after he and Danita had left the next morning? He had to try to find it.

Ten minutes turned into fifteen, and still no cabin had appeared. How was that possible? After a half hour, Griffin admitted that the cabin itself might have been a portal to the Fey realm as Kenton claimed. Damn.

He turned around and headed back to the eternal flame, needing to speak with one of the Forresters. When he arrived, both visiting families were gone. Good. All alone, he stepped up to the flame and waited for someone in the family to appear.

The flames flickered, sending soothing warmth toward him. When no one showed up, he called out to Bevon, but he didn't appear either. Were they avoiding him?

His gut churned. If something had happened to Tory, Bevon might have returned to the realm to help out. That didn't explain Fay's absence though.

Shit. After an hour of no contact, Griffin headed back down the path. Just as he reached the open field, Fay stepped out in front of him. "Griffin."

"Fay. I've been waiting to speak with one of you."

"I know."

What did that mean? "Do you have any news about Tory?"

"She'll be fine."

"Have you visited her?"

Fay smiled. "No."

Griffin didn't like the short answers. Fay was hiding something. "Do you think you could check on her condition for me?"

As a Guardian, he could create a portal to Earth in a few seconds. He imagined she could do the same to her realm.

Fay placed a hand on his arm. "Don't you trust my brothers?"

If he said he didn't, and Kenton turned out to be a good guy, Griffin would feel like a cad. "Can you speculate when she might be returned?"

"When Kenton says she is ready to come back."

Clearly, Fay wasn't going to tell him anything. "If you hear of anything, let me know."

Of course, neither he nor anyone in his family had ever been contacted by a member of the Forrester family, but he could hope. They only spoke when one of the Guardians visited the eternal flame—or in the case of Fay, when she'd attended Birk and Lily's wedding.

She nodded and then disintegrated into tiny points of light. He thought that rather passive aggressive of her, but he should just be thankful she and her brother had cured Danita. For that he would be eternally grateful.

On the other hand, if Kenton never returned with Tory, he and his family might have to wage war against the Forresters.

DANITA STRETCHED AND then opened her eyes. She couldn't believe how well she'd slept. When she rolled over to say hello to Griffin, she found herself alone in bed. "Griffin?" she called.

The bathroom was dark, implying he must be in the kitchen. It was only eight, so she doubted he'd have gone into work already. In case Wendy was already up, Danita rolled out of bed and dressed for the day. When she'd finished, she stepped into the main room.

"Wendy! What are you doing?"

Her cousin turned from the stove and smiled. "I woke up early and decided to cook you some breakfast."

"That is so sweet of you. Have you seen Griffin?"

Wendy nodded to the piece of paper on the counter. Danita read it. "He went to speak with Bevon Forrester. I guess I shouldn't be surprised. Griffin needs answers."

"He's still upset I take it?"

Danita pulled out the barstool and sat. "Yes. He is being stubborn though. There is no reason for him to think anything that happened was his fault. Sure, he should be sad that Tory was injured and then infected, but if he hadn't let Kenton help her, she might have died. If that had happened, he really would have hated himself for life."

"I agree. It was really strange. She fell from the sky in her dragon form, but a minute later, she shifted and then stood up. I thought she was going to be fine. Malpan grabbed her, and Tory dropped to the ground like a dead weight. A second later, Kenton sort of threw Malpan into that portal." Her cousin scooped out the eggs and placed them on a plate next to a piece of toast. "It's not much. Your fridge could use some stocking."

"No kidding. I have to go shopping."

To an outsider, it would seem as if the conversation about Tory had been dismissed, but Danita knew her caring cousin. It was her way of hinting that Danita should not dwell on what she couldn't control. For now, she'd go along with it.

Wendy placed a plate in front of Danita while she stood at the kitchen counter and then shoveled a large bite into her mouth. "Mmm. I have to say, I did a good job."

That made Danita smile. "You did."

Wendy waved a fork at her. "All bragging aside, I can't thank you enough for letting me stay here last night. I really felt safe."

"Of course. You can stay for as long as you need, you know," Danita told her.

"I appreciate that, but I would feel more comfortable in my own place. Besides, my computer is there. While being held captive, my mind was soaring with stories. I'll be busy for weeks putting down all my thoughts."

Danita was happy for her cousin. "Are you going to do an exposé on Malpan and his slaves?"

"I want to, but I don't like to mention people without their permission. It's possible those who had been held captive might not want the world to know that they'd been mind controlled. In order to ask them though, I need to learn their names." She chuckled. "I believe Griffin's brother—Logan is his name—was asking them for their information."

"When I see Griffin, I'll see what he knows." Danita shivered. "That's considerate of you to ask permission. If you can't get a hold of them, or they say no, you can always write about your experience. I would ask one favor though."

"What's that?"

"That you speak with Griffin first to see if he has a problem with you discussing the reason for Malpan coming after the Caspians."

"I can do that."

Once they finished their meal, Wendy said she needed to return home. "I'll bring these clothes back after I wash them."

"Take your time."

"And you? What are you going to do today? I hope not chase after Griffin."

She had thought about it. "Bevon lives in the middle of the realm. That would take me hours to drive there. By then, Griffin could be back home. No, I want to see if Logan can give me any helpful hints about how to help his brother."

"With his guilt?"

"Yes."

"Good luck."

They hugged goodbye. Once Wendy was gone, Danita cleaned up the breakfast dishes. Since Griffin was apparently on his quest for answers, she headed to Caspian Mines to pick Logan's brain.

Chapter Twenty-One

W HEN DANITA WALKED into Logan's office, he looked up from his desk, set down his pen, and smiled. "Hey. How's Wendy?"

He pushed back his chair and came around to the front of his desk, motioning they sit on the sofa.

"Good. Real good, in fact. She wasn't infected with any kind of dark magic, but being cooped up in a dirty mine all by herself would break anyone. But not Wendy. She's amazing. In fact, she wants to interview some of the slaves to ask their permission to write about them."

His eyes widened. "Given she had been snooping around Malpan's affairs, I guess she's the type to do anything to get the story. It's in a journalist's blood."

Danita smiled. "That's true, but deep inside I believe she is still raw from the experience. This is probably her way of coping."

"It probably is. How is Griffin holding up? I've been texting him on and off since he flew Wendy back to your place, but he hasn't answered."

"He's hurting."

Logan leaned back and blew out a breath. "He told me what happened to Tory. Knowing my carry-the-weight-on-his-shoulders brother, he thinks he shouldn't have caved so easily."

"You know him well."

"I do, but in all honesty, Griffin already said as much and asked me to tell Kaleena, Declan, and Ramsey what happened."

"He spoke to her parents last night."

"How did that go?"

"They seemed to have understood, but that didn't give him any peace of mind."

"I'm not surprised," Logan said. "What can I help you with today?"

"I came in part because I wanted to see if you had any suggestions."

"Suggestions?"

She huffed. "How to convince Griffin not to be so hard on himself."

Logan smiled. "You figure that out, and I'll give you a gold medal."

"I'm serious."

Logan held up a hand. "Okay. Our best hope is that Tory walks in here later today or tomorrow. Then all will be well."

"And if she doesn't?"

"If that doesn't happen, maybe suggest to Grif that the two of you go on a small vacation—someplace quiet where you can, shall we say, distract him."

A guy would suggest that. "As nice as that sounds, your brother won't go for it."

"Okay then. What about talking to the Forresters and asking them when Tory will be back? I thought Bevon was a stand-up guy. I didn't interact with Kenton, but Stone did. My sister Nessa and my brother Birk speak highly of Fay."

"That's where Griffin went this morning."

Logan whistled. "I hope he doesn't get violent."

"Griffin would never do that. The Forresters healed me."

"Only joking, but if they don't give him the answer he wants, his mood might worsen."

Great. "Now I know what Griffin went through all those months when I was moody and dejected, because of the darkness that was inside of me. I know how destructive that can be to both parties."

Logan reached out and clasped her hand. "Give him time. He'll come around."

"I hope so."

The outside door clicked, and Logan stood. "I'll be right back. I sense a shifter, and it's not of the dragon kind. Stay here."

Really? Danita truly believed that the danger was finally past, and that she and Griffin could get on with their lives. Not that she knew what the future held exactly, but at the very least, Danita hoped she could go back to her old job of being an accountant. She'd quit only because the darkness had been eating away at her.

A moment later, Logan returned to the office with Wendy in tow, grinning ear to ear. Okay, this was a surprise.

"Look who I found," he said.

Danita jumped up. "Wendy! Is anything wrong?"

"No. I mentioned that I wanted to speak with some of the men who'd been held captive, but then I realized I had no idea where they are now," she said acting unusually flirty. "I then remembered that Logan had a list of their names."

Before he could answer, Griffin came through the door with his lips pressed firmly together and his eyes slightly narrowed. Not good. On the bright side, anger was easier to deal with than depression. Wanting to show him that she was there for him, she opened her arms and embraced him. "How did it go?" she asked, though she could guess.

"Not as well as I'd hoped." His hug wasn't as intense as usual either. Damn.

She wasn't sure how much he wanted Wendy to learn about the other Feys. "Wendy came to ask about the men who were in the mines. She wants to find them."

"I'd like to speak with them too," Griffin said.

"Why?" Danita understood Wendy's desire.

"Right before we'd finished rounding up the prisoners, I noticed Bevon was sorting the freed men into groups according to which province they were from." He ground out his words. "I want to know what Bevon told them."

"Why? His actions seem like he was trying to help get them back home," Danita said.

"I thought so too, but something is up with that family."

Logan swung around a chair and motioned Wendy sit down. Griffin led Danita to the small sofa where she and Logan had been seated, while his brother leaned a hip on the edge of his desk.

"I take it you learned something today that made you an irritable old grouch," Logan said.

She swore one corner of Griffin's lips turned up. Go, Logan.

"Yes and no." He explained how none of the Forrester family had been home. Using the word *home* instead of forest implied he didn't want Wendy to have too many details.

"I told Wendy all about Meena showing me to the cabin in the woods," Danita added, hoping that would help.

"Good. The fact remains they weren't there. I found that quite suspicious. When I was leaving the forest though, Fay showed up. All she would say was that Tory would be okay. I asked if she'd spoken to Kenton or Bevon, and she said no. Basically, she blew me off."

"Bro, she might just know that her brother can help Tory. I say we give her a few more days before we go back and storm the place."

Griffin huffed. "You know me well." He leaned back in the seat. "Fine. I'll wait, but I won't like it."

Danita rubbed his leg, trying to calm him. Thankfully, she caught a few teal swirls swimming in his eyes.

"About the captured men?" Wendy asked.

Logan looked over at her. "I don't know how much they will be able to help. After Griffin took you back to town, we finished rounding up the rest of the twenty-five men. Bevon spent a minute with each of them and then told us where they each lived. I jotted down the information. The problem was that when I delivered the first of my two men to the shelter in Edendale, they had no idea why I was carrying them."

Danita glanced between Griffin and Wendy, but they didn't

seem to understand either. "Did you tell them you'd saved them from having been captured for a few weeks or rather months?"

"Yup. Mind you I wasn't looking for any gratitude. A small thank you would have been nice though. It was as if whatever they'd gone through never registered in their brain."

"What about the others?" Danita asked, her curiosity peaked.

"I returned five men to Avonbelle Province, while Stone, Thane, Camden, and Finn returned the rest to the other three provinces. I finished first, so I helped Stone take two of his group to Thedia. It was the same thing. They remembered where they lived, but not that they'd been held captive. Stone asked them if they knew what month it was, and they got it wrong."

"Bevon must have erased their memory," Danita said. "Where was he when I needed him?" She waved a hand. "In all honesty, forgetting wouldn't have helped remove my darkness. It might have made it worse if I didn't understand it."

Griffin clasped her hand. "Do you know any white lighters who can do that kind of spell—erase a person's memory?"

"No, but Kenton and Bevon are Fey. We have no idea what their talents are. I mean, I saw Meena turn into points of light. Don't tell me that's not strange."

"You might be right."

Wendy slapped her thighs and stood. "I'd still like to speak with the two men Logan carried to the shelter. I was there with them. It's possible they didn't know they could trust you guys and are keeping quiet."

"If their minds hadn't been erased, they might just have shoved the trauma down so deeply that they don't want to remember," Danita said. "I know of what I speak." Griffin squeezed her hand and then let go.

"You know me, Danita. I'm stubborn," Wendy said. "I never stop digging."

Danita chuckled. "That's true. It's why the two of us get along so well. We're both the same."

Logan stood. "I'll take you to the shelter where the men are staying."

Danita hadn't expected that, but from the smile on her cousin's face, she certainly didn't mind.

"We'll join you," Griffin added. "I want to know what that Bevon character told the men."

"I bet they won't remember," Danita said. "It's how spells work. Don't get me wrong, I still think we should speak with them."

Not only did her cousin need to see for herself that these men remembered nothing, Danita wanted to be there for them if they did recall being slaves in a mine.

"Are we going to fly?" Wendy asked sounding way too excited.

Logan glanced over at Griffin. "Your call."

"If Danita is okay with it."

"I am." By now being carried had become second nature to Danita. If she and Griffin did mate, and if she did inherit his ability to shift, she wasn't sure she wanted to learn though. Being on her own in the sky scared her. Besides, she wasn't ready to give up that warm, cozy feeling of being in his grasp.

Logan stepped next to Wendy. "You've been carried by a dragon before, right?"

She shook her head. "But I'm not afraid."

Logan's grin said it all. He liked her. Danita clasped Griffin's hand, and they stepped outside. Both men walked a good distance away from the building and shifted.

Wendy leaned over. "Is Logan hot or what? My wolf is going crazy."

Too bad Wendy often made that comment. "He's very cute."

Wendy sobered. "I bet he's married, isn't he? I always like the married ones."

"No. To my knowledge, he isn't seeing anyone either."

Her eyes sparkled. "That's too good to be true."

Logan stood to his full height. Really? If Danita didn't know better, she'd think he was showing off. A moment later, he swooped closer and picked up Wendy. Her cousin's eyes and mouth opened wide, but Danita didn't detect any fear. Given what Wendy had gone through recently, Danita was impressed with her cousin's ability to experience any kind of joy.

As soon as they shot upward, Griffin took Danita in his grasp and followed them. Danita leaned her head back and closed her eyes, loving the feeling of freedom. With her darkness gone, she was ready to embrace life.

All too soon, they landed on top of the SinCas building. With all of the hustle and bustle on the street and sidewalks below, this was the best place to land. She had no idea where the shelter was located, but wherever it was, as long as she was with Griffin, she'd be happy.

Logan set Wendy down at the same time Danita's feet touched the roof. Both men shifted.

Wendy turned to her. "I know you said it was quite the experience, but that was amazing."

Wendy hugged her. Danita didn't know what that was for, but she was just thrilled Wendy seemed so well-adjusted after her ordeal.

"Ready, ladies?" Logan asked with a lot of cheer in his voice.

"Yes." Wendy stepped next to Logan. Okay, clearly her cousin was smitten.

It took about seven minutes by foot to reach the shelter. Logan had all of the men's names and their addresses—assuming they had one. Many were homeless—like the two they were about to visit.

Once inside the shelter, Logan said he'd find the men for them. Five minutes later, both men came out and looked around, appearing to still be in a daze. Surely, Logan told them why they were there.

Wendy stepped up to them and held out her hand. "Hi, I'm Wendy Oprander. I was with you two in the mine."

As they shook her hand, the two men looked at each other. "The mine?" the shorter of the two said.

This was worse than Danita thought. It did appear as if their minds had been erased.

Griffin stepped up to them. "If you wouldn't mind giving us a moment of your time, we have a few questions." He held out some Denlars to each of them, which the men quickly snatched up.

"Sure. Name's Eddie Lawson. What do you need to know?"

At least he remembered his name. "What did you do yesterday?" Griffin asked.

Eddie looked over at the other man. It was almost as if he needed the support, or else he was hiding something. "I somehow landed deep in some woods with a bunch of other guys." Eddie had nodded to Logan. "Then this guy here shifts into a dragon and flies me back here."

"You don't remember what you've been doing for the last five months?" Wendy asked.

"I...ah... have a habit of blacking out, but I've never been this gone before. Right, Joe?"

Joe nodded. "The last thing I remember was I'd found this used tent in the park. It was in the trash, so I took it. This summer has been bitchin' hot, and I wanted to have some shelter from the sun."

This past summer's heat had been the worst in history. But summer ended a few months ago. "You don't remember working in a mine?" Danita asked.

Joe laughed. "Me? No, ma'am. It's my life goal to do as little work as I can."

Wendy blew out a breath. "Thank you for your time."

Danita understood how much this story meant to Wendy, but they weren't going to learn anything by hanging around so all four of them left.

"I don't suspect the other men will know more," Danita said once they were outside.

Logan shook his head. "They all seemed confused as to why they were grouped together in the woods." He glanced between them. "How about we share a coffee and pastry at Angelique's? My treat."

Wendy's eyes sparkled. "Thank you, Logan. I'd love that. That is so nice of you."

Danita almost laughed. She'd never acted like that with Griffin. Ever. Then again, Danita wasn't a shifter, so maybe Wendy knew something Danita hadn't.

Chapter Twenty-Two

AFTER THEIR FLIGHT back to Caspian Mines in order for Wendy to pick up her car, Danita hugged her cousin goodbye and then told Griffin she needed to run a few errands.

"Are you feeling okay?" he asked, acting all protective again.

"Yes. I need to go shopping and stuff." She'd thought that after Malpan was caught, Griffin wouldn't be so protective—not that she minded—but apparently she'd been wrong. "I also want to find a real job. Not having the darkness inside me makes me feel like my old self again." She smiled to assure him all was well.

He grinned, leaned over, and kissed her. "Good luck."

"Thank you. See you for dinner then?"

"I will be there."

As soon as Griffin stepped back inside, she left. While Danita planned to speak with her former boss about a letter of recommendation, her main reason for wanting to leave was that she planned to make Griffin an amazing dinner. He'd been so focused on taking down Malpan and finding Wendy and the slaves, that they hadn't had the time to enjoy each other's company—other than in the bedroom.

Sure, he was still out of sorts over Tory's temporary displacement, but she believed his cousin would return as healthy as ever. The question was when.

On the way to the grocery store, Danita stopped at Dr. Aminor's office. While she assumed the good doctor would be busy with a client, Danita wanted to let the secretary know that she needed to cancel Danita's weekly standing appointment. *Thank you, Kenton.*

As soon as she stepped inside the reception area, the door to Dr. Aminor's office opened, and a middle-aged man exited her office. Her therapist looked up, and her brows pinched in concern. "Danita, is everything all right?"

"Yes." There was another woman sitting in the reception room, but since this office served two therapists, Danita couldn't tell if she was meeting with Dr. Aminor or Dr. Heldspell.

"Would you like to come in?" Dr. Aminor asked.

"Just for a sec." Danita didn't want to take up her time. It also wouldn't be fair to Griffin for him to pay for a session she no longer needed.

"Have a seat," Dr. Aminor said.

"I just came to tell you I no longer need any more sessions."

"Is that so? What has changed?"

As succinctly as possible, Danita explained about having met someone who had removed the darkness inside her. "I am feeling incredible now. Not only that, Griffin, the man who helped me, found Wendy. She is doing really well too. Added to all my joy is that Griffin and I are together." Heat raced up her face. "I'm actually living with him."

The joy in Dr. Aminor's eyes appeared sincere. "I couldn't be happier, but it all happened so fast. You were just in here."

"I know, but once the darkness disappeared, things moved fast after that."

They chatted a bit more, and then Danita stood. "Thank you for everything. I need to get going though. I'm making a big dinner for Griffin tonight. It's been a long time since I've felt like cooking."

Dr. Aminor came around her desk and hugged Danita. "I wish you the best of luck."

"Thank you."

After Danita left, she headed to the store to pick up some groceries for the surprise meal she would be making for Griffin. Once home, she shot off an email to her old boss explaining that after extensive therapy, she was back to normal, and that she was looking for a job again. If he could write a letter of recommendation, she'd appreciate it.

Right now, Danita had never been better. The only shadow hanging over them was Tory. If she didn't return, it would forever haunt the man Danita had fallen in love with.

Not wanting to dwell on negative thoughts, especially today, she went about making her spinach lasagna. It wasn't fancy, but she was sure it would please Griffin. She would make a tossed salad with goat cheese and pine nuts, along with some nutty bread, and the meal would be a smash. No doubt they'd end up in bed, ready to celebrate him saving so many people—which was her plan all along.

Danita set the table and even put on a silky crimson dress—something she hadn't done in a long time either. Bringing cheer to Griffin was her goal. And it wasn't just because he'd done so much for her. She loved him, plain and simple.

When he didn't arrive home by five thirty, she began to worry. The dinner had just finished cooking, so she removed it from the oven. To her delight, the moment she set it on the counter, Griffin walked in.

His wide eyes and grin told her she had impressed him. Danita was also taken aback when Griffin handed her a bouquet of flowers and a bag from a store called Helpful Healing.

"For you." He smiled and waved a hand at the table. "I see we had the same idea about needing to celebrate."

"Yes, but you didn't have to give me gifts," she said as she set the flowers and bag on the counter.

"I did. I've been such a grouch lately that I wanted to make it up to you. You definitely deserve better than that."

"Aw." She wrapped her arms around his neck, and then kissed him.

"Hmm. Remind me to bring you flowers more often."

"You know you don't have to give me anything to win my heart."

"I know, but I'd like to if it makes you happy." He closed his eyes and inhaled. "Dinner smells divine."

Danita stepped away. "It's a recipe I've not made for you before. I decided to whip it up because I wanted to celebrate you finding Wendy and helping free the men." She purposefully didn't mention Tory. Danita was convinced they'd be reunited with her soon.

He moved closer. "Thank you." He dragged a hand down to her waist. "I love the dress. I don't think I've ever seen you in one before."

She was thrilled he noticed. "I went home and grabbed one. It's not my usual style, but I wanted to make things nice for you. You worked hard to find and then free the men in the mine. And now you have."

He tapped her nose. "I had a lot of help—help that first came from a very special lady." He nodded to the flowers. "How about putting them in water while I change? We can eat and then...well... we'll figure out something to do."

He winked and then ducked into the bedroom. Something good must have happened during the day to have caused his mood change. Whatever it was, she was happy about it.

When Danita searched for a vase to put the flowers in, all she could find was a water pitcher. Once they made things more permanent, she wanted to do a little decorating, as well as add to his sorely lacking supply of kitchen gear. The place could use a woman's touch for sure.

She put the food on the table and lit the candles. The bedroom door opened. He'd changed into a tight white T-shirt and jeans. No socks. No belt. And from the outline of his cock pressed against his jeans, no briefs. Score. They definitely were on the same page tonight.

He looked over at the table. "This is incredible. All I can think of right now is making love with you, but I know you went to a lot of trouble preparing this meal. How about we eat? As in right now. If we wait, I'm not sure I can keep my distance from you for much longer. My dragon is already turning feisty."

Danita loved it when Griffin acted desperate to be with her. Sitting across from each other, he poured their wine and then held up his glass. She tapped hers to his. "What should we toast to?" she asked.

"To us!"

She had thought he'd refer to the successful mission, but she liked his toast better. "To us."

They both dug in. "This is incredible," Griffin said. "I should have asked you to move in a long time ago."

He seemed to be fighting a smile. "Smart ass."

"What? I thought you said you liked to cook."

"I do."

Not wanting to spoil the romantic mood, Danita took a bite of the lasagna, and then the salad, and finally the bread. Everything was perfect. When she looked up at Griffin, he was devouring the meal, acting as if he hadn't eaten in days. Either that, or he truly couldn't wait to reach the bedroom. That worked for her.

He looked up with food in his mouth and kind of smiled. Griffin held up a finger and chewed before swallowing. "Sorry."

"Don't be. I'm glad you are enjoying it."

"I want to enjoy your company more."

She'd guessed it. "I wanted to share with you that I stopped by Dr. Aminor's office today and told her that I no longer needed her services."

He set down his fork. "That's fantastic. Did you speak with your old boss too?"

"I sent him an email asking for a recommendation. And of course, I cooked. You?"

Danita didn't ask for specifics, but something good must have happened today. He was in a particularly good mood.

"After I contacted our clients and told them about Malpan and his illegal mine, they all agreed to buy their copper from us."

Danita clapped. The success of Caspian Mines meant so much to him. "That's wonderful."

"Thanks." With his plate clean and his wine glass empty, he pushed back his chair. "What would make it an even better day would be if you joined me in the bedroom. I've been fantasizing all day about making love with you."

"Is that so? And you think flowers and…oh, no. I never opened my gift."

"It can wait," he said as he came around the table.

"I have to open it. I don't want to be distracted when I'm undressing and doing other entertaining things."

"Trust me, once I start kissing and touching you, you won't be thinking about the present."

Where had this flirty charming man come from? While she was certain he was still quite upset over Tory, he was doing a good job of hiding it.

"That's true, but just give me a sec." Danita stepped over to the counter and opened the bag. "Awesome! A salt lamp. I've always wanted one." It was yellow orange. "I'm kind of glad this one wasn't made from sardonyx. That would have reminded me of that terrible Changeling werewolf from Earth."

With his gaze on her, Griffin slipped it out of her hands and placed it on the counter. "That's why I bought the yellow one. It will help calm us, but right now, being calm isn't on my mind."

"What is on your mind?" she asked, trying to act innocent.

"This." Griffin reached behind her back and unzipped her red dress.

Wouldn't he be surprised when he found out she had nothing underneath? He slipped the dress off her shoulders and the material dropped to the floor. Every one of his dragon responses flared. His eyes not only turned teal, but they became laced with gold and orange streaks. His teeth elongated too, and it seemed as if every cell in his body flashed rust.

"You are incredible," Griffin said, and then wet his lips, as her dress exposed her naked body—all except for her high heels.

"Thank you. Now that I'm almost undressed, how about you

showing me yours?"

Danita often asked to be the one to undress him, but this time she was too excited to take the time.

"My pleasure." Wearing only two pieces of clothing, he ditched them in seconds. "I can't even decide where to begin," he said as he ran his gaze up and down her body.

"If you follow me, I'm thinking you can figure it out." With her high heels clicking on the tile floor, Danita sashayed into the bedroom. Because Wendy had been at the condo this morning, Danita hadn't taken the time to make the bed. Just as well. Rolling around in freshly slept-in sheets was more decadent anyway.

She was halfway there when Griffin lifted her up and deposited her on the cool sheets. Like a lion on the prowl, he climbed on top of her. "Danita Warren. I know I've already told you before, but I want to say it again—I love you, and I want to spend the rest of my life with you. To do that involves the two of us fully mating."

She grinned. "If you are asking my permission to make me yours, then I say yes."

"I was hoping you'd agree." The kisses that followed were the best ever. It was as if all of Griffin's worries from the last few months had been forgotten. He broke the kiss and slid down, his hands cupping her shoulders and then finding her breasts. "I could drown in these."

He was being silly, but she loved him even more for it. "Enjoy."

"Oh, I plan to." And enjoy them he did if his moans were any indication.

With the sucking and pulling motion of his lips on her nipples, her pussy vibrated with need. Knowing they would soon be one made this lovemaking extra special. Never in her life had Danita believed that anyone would love her so much, nor did she believe she'd find someone as remarkable as Griffin Caspian. Now she had.

On the next tug, she clamped down hard on his shoulders and nearly drowned in her own bliss that was streaking pleasure through her. Running her hands up and down his shoulders, she imagined the two of them floating, as if they were making love in the sky.

He pressed her breasts together while he dragged his teeth across her distended nipples. It was too much, and her climax brimmed.

"I need to taste you as well," she panted. *Or I might explode too soon.*

Without complaint, he rose to his knees, looking magnificent. How did she get so lucky? Danita rolled over to his side, lifted up onto her knees, and then bent over. The first swipe of her tongue energized her, and she swore she started to glow from the inside. The light didn't come from any scales, but rather from her own internal happiness. That had never happened before—but then she'd never been in love while being cleansed of darkness either.

She must have slightly stiffened, because Griffin rubbed her back. "It means you are ready, Danita. It's natural."

Could he read her mind? Even if he could, it didn't matter. He was right. She wanted to be with Griffin. Needing more of him, she opened her mouth wide and lowered her lips. When the end of his cock hit the back of her throat, she swirled her tongue around and around. His scales flashed and his nails sharpened. Taking a hold of him, she pumped her fist.

"Enough," he ground out a few seconds later.

He swung around so that he was behind her. "I plan to mate with you tonight, Danita."

"I can't wait."

Chapter Twenty-Three

WHEN GRIFFIN PRESSED his cock against her opening and remained still for a few seconds, Danita thought it was because he needed to center himself. But what did she know? All she could be certain of was that she wanted to be with him forever.

Leaning over her, he palmed her tits and pressed them together. Then his lips found her neck. Instead of the expected bite, he kissed her from shoulder to ear. "I love you," he whispered.

Those gentle, yet powerful, words helped relax her. It wasn't as if she wasn't aware of what needed to happen for them to mate, but she didn't know how her body would react. "I love you more."

"Don't play that game of who has the upper hand. Just know that I am the powerful Griffin Caspian."

That was so ridiculous coming from him that she actually chuckled. To her surprise though, the tension in her body disappeared. Knowing him, he had done it on purpose.

Griffin ran his hands down the sides of her body and then held her hips still. With slow deliberation, he eased into her, acting as if she were fragile, which was definitely not the case. She wished she could prove it to him.

The fact remained that Griffin would always be her protector. For all she knew, he thought the glow coming off of her body meant she'd shatter. She might, but only because her love for him was that immense.

Griffin withdrew and then drove right back in, sending spikes of lust up and down her spine. His heated body covering hers, coupled with the way his breaths had increased, pushed her climax closer. For some inexplicable reason, she wanted to hold out a little bit longer—just until they mated.

He withdrew and then stilled. While she couldn't see his flashing scales, she suspected he was working hard not to take her before he believed she was ready.

"Mate with me, damn it," she demanded. Desperate to show him just how much she wanted him, Danita pressed her hips back.

His grip tightened. "Are you trying to tell me how you want it, lady?" he asked.

This time she almost laughed out loud. "Dumb question. You know I want it any way I can get it, as long as it is only with you."

"Then you shall have it."

As if she'd finally given her consent, he drove back in again. This time after he withdrew, he tunneled in again and again, taking her to new heights. His now sharp teeth hovered over her skin. She lowered her head, providing ample space for him to bite her.

He let go of one hip and moved her hair out of the way. This was it. The moment she'd thought about for quite a while.

Danita expected him to bite her right away, but instead he wrapped his arms around her waist and pulled her close as he continued to make love with her. Each time the tip of his cock hit the end, swells of desire built.

"I'm close," she panted. Danita almost didn't want this perfect moment to end, but her body wasn't listening.

"So am I, my love."

With that, his teeth sunk into her neck. While she barely felt the pinch, her body took on a glow of its own, entombing them both in its light. It was as if he was transferring all of his energy into her, including his love. Her climax added to the existing intensity, sweeping her away and nearly blinding her.

Then all sounds ceased to exist, and Danita was forced to open her mouth to inhale sufficient oxygen. His cock detonated, and he let out a primal yell. She swore it sounded like some ancient dragon ancestor finally coming to life.

The next thing she was aware of was his tongue licking her neck. Only then did her body finally give way. Her knees collapsed, and she dropped onto her stomach. A moment later, Griffin was on his back with her on top.

"Are you okay?" he asked. Once more his protective nature colored his voice.

She stroked his face. "More than okay. That was beyond anything I ever could have imagined."

He tugged her close and held her tight. Between the wine and the lovemaking, she fell asleep more content than she ever had been before.

THE NEXT FEW days were pure bliss. Okay, that wasn't totally true. The sex was perfect, but during the day, Griffin sort of slipped back into his worry mode about Tory. Once more Logan had to talk Griffin out of returning to the eternal flame to look for the Forresters. Sometimes, it was best to leave things alone.

It didn't seem to matter that the Caspian sales of copper were back to normal—or to be more specific, better than normal—since they had picked up a lot of the customers from Malpan. More customers meant a higher production need, and Caspian Mines actually had to hire more men.

Griffin wasn't in charge of that part of the business, but Logan was. Griffin said that Logan had been seriously busy with a constant influx of men looking for work. Unless they found someone to take over Malpan's mine, the people who worked there would be out of a job soon.

While she was having fun bouncing between Angelique's coffee shop, chatting with Wendy along with a lot of other friends, and stopping in at the Caspian Mines, she was holding her breath waiting on word from her old boss. Until she heard from him, she didn't want to apply someplace else, especially since she didn't have a recommendation in hand.

Tomorrow she would stop in to see him. It was always possible, her boss never received her email. She refused to believe he was blowing her off.

Tonight Griffin said he wanted to take her out to dinner. He refused to say why, but she didn't care. She loved being with him, and ever since they'd mated, her need for him had grown by leaps and bounds.

Her cell rang. It was Griffin, and she smiled. "Hey there."

"Hey. I'm going to have to stay a little later at work, and I thought it might be faster if you came here. Then we can go to dinner together."

She hadn't been ready to learn to fly—or shift—yet, so she still had to rely on Griffin to carry her places whenever they didn't drive. Given her history with having all the dark light inside of her, she feared she would fail at that. "Sure. Where are we going?" She didn't want to dress too casually if they were going to a fancy place.

"I thought the Highlanders' Steakhouse."

Ooh. Fancy. "Perfect. I'll change and head over."

Excited, Danita searched through her drawers for the perfect underwear. It became evident that laundry was in her near future, but she did find her white lace bra. Interestingly enough, Griffin seemed to treat her a bit differently when she wore white. He told her she looked pure and more chaste in it. Little did he know! Danita giggled to herself. Actually he did know, and he was the reason she wasn't innocent anymore.

Once she changed, she slipped into a navy blue dress. In case it was chilly in the restaurant, she grabbed a cute Kelly green sweater. When she checked the mirror, Danita smiled. She never used to think that she looked hot in anything she wore. Now, she realized that she did and attributed it all to Griffin.

Not wanting to keep him waiting, she rushed down the hall and took the elevator to the underground parking. A girl could definitely get used to this luxury. Danita was hoping that tonight he'd ask her to move in permanently. After all, that was what mating was all about, right?

The drive seemed to take forever, but when she arrived at the mine, she hopped out and rushed inside. It was after hours. The receptionist had gone home, and no one seemed to be about, so she headed to Griffin's office. As she neared the closed door, her body ignited with need. Whoa. Her desires were becoming more and more out of control, even when they weren't touching. Griffin said it would take a bit of time to learn how to handle all of the lust. Right now, she wasn't sure she'd ever figure out how to control it.

As for the rest of the changes, she hadn't looked in the mirror when they were making love, but Griffin often mentioned how much he liked her purple eyes. To him, that meant she was now all dragon shifter. She wasn't so sure. Her skin didn't flash a color, but he said that once she shifted, it would appear.

She knocked on his door and then entered. Griffin looked up and smiled. "Hey. Wow. You look hot. Another dress! I'm liking this trend."

Heat raced up her face, mostly because Logan was there.

"Hey, Danita. You do look nice."

"Thanks, Logan."

Griffin's brother looked back at him. "We'll finish up tomorrow, okay?"

Now she felt bad. She hadn't come to cut short Griffin's work-day, but he had asked her to meet him there. "I can wait in the break room."

"No. If I stayed," Logan continued, "we might be at it for hours."

As he moved past her toward the door, Kenton filled the frame. She hadn't even heard his footsteps, and her hearing was now amazingly good. Her heart sang that he'd returned from wherever he lived. That might mean Tory was here!

Her joy was short lived when the man who'd helped remove her darkness frowned.

Griffin jumped up. "You're back. Where's Tory? Is she okay?"

"Yes. She's in her apartment, but I need to tell you something first. Please, will all of you take a seat?"

Griffin's lips firmed, but from the way his body had stiffened, she couldn't tell if he wanted to strangle Kenton or hug him. She believed the former, though she personally was excited that he'd come. He'd have information. The fact Tory was at her apartment sounded like good news—unless she hadn't recovered, and the darkness was still in her.

Griffin pulled over two chairs and motioned she take a seat. He sat next to her while Logan dropped down on the loveseat.

"Tell us," Griffin said.

"The extraction process took longer than I had hoped. Bevon helped, but we had to call in some other favors. All that matters in the end is that Tory has been healed completely. All of Malpan's evilness is gone."

Danita reached over and clasped Griffin's hand. "That is good news. I hear a *but* coming."

"Not a but, exactly, but a request."

"What kind of request," Griffin asked, the tension around his eyes almost gone.

"I ask that you not tell Tory about her visit to Feyrion."

Griffin looked first at Danita and then at Logan. "How do you propose we do that? She was there. She'd know what happened."

"About that. You see some of us have the ability to erase some events from a person's mind. I don't think my parents were too thrilled that I took Tory to Feyrion to heal her, so I had no choice but to block those memories."

"Why can't we tell her?" Griffin asked.

"For the same reason you don't want people on Earth to know your realm exists."

He had a point.

"Are you expecting us to lie to her then?" Griffin asked, his lips pressed thin.

"Not lie, per se. Just say nothing. With her memory of her time on Feyrion deleted, she'll remember going to the mine that day, sneaking inside, and then opening the big stone door. She told me about the fight she had, and how she'd fallen. The next thing she will remember—when you wake her up—is that Declan and Greer healed her. I would appreciate you asking them for their help in keeping the story consistent."

Griffin stood. "Done." He held out his hand. "I am grateful for you healing her and returning her safely. May we see her?"

"That's why I came. Bevon is with her now. Once you arrive, we will leave. I only ask that after you wake her up, you explain to her how ill she has been. You can even say that Malpan infected her with his evilness, and that it took all of Declan's and Greer's abilities to heal her. She won't even know we helped in any way."

From his wistful eyes, he wished the outcome had been different.

"Consider it done."

"I'll meet you there and let Bevon know you are on your way."

"I take it you don't need a lift?" Griffin asked Kenton.

When the man smiled, his face lit up. "No. I have my own method of transportation."

A second later he was gone. It would take Danita a while to get used to being around someone who could teleport. She stood. "I think that is fantastic news." Griffin turned toward her, surprising her that he had worry lines around his mouth. She thought he was okay with everything. While she couldn't read his mind, she could guess what he was thinking. "Don't do this, Griffin."

"Do what?'

"Second guess yourself. If you had insisted she remain on Tarradon, she'd have that darkness in her for life. Do you really want her to have to go through the nightmares, the doubt, and the constant fear, like I did?"

His face softened, and then he stepped in front of her. Griffin gathered her in his powerful arms, and his warmth soothed her. "You are right. It is the best outcome."

She leaned back. "What are we waiting for? Let's go see Tory."

Griffin addressed Logan. "I know you want to come with us, but if she remembers very little, it might be hard to explain why all three of us are hovering over her when she opens her eyes."

Logan held up a hand. "You two go. I'll check up on her tomorrow. In the meantime, I'll let Kaleena know that her sister is okay. I'll also coach her on what to say. I'll do the same for Declan and Greer."

"That would be great." Griffin squeezed Danita's waist. "Come on. We don't want to keep Kenton waiting."

Thrilled that Griffin seemed to have overcome his frustration, they exited out the front. "You sure you don't want to try to shift?" he asked.

"And possibly ruin my dress if my dragon comes out too quickly?" She was kidding—mostly—but she thought it best to lighten the mood.

He smiled, just as she'd hoped. "You win."

He shifted and then swooped her up in his arms. It took all of three minutes to reach the building where Tory lived. He landed on the roof and shifted with not even a hair out of place. How did he do that? He'd told her it was magic, but it seemed more than that.

They entered the stairwell. "It's going to be hard not to spill the beans," she said. "Can we say that Kenton took Malpan back to his realm at least?"

"We'll have to ask him. I'd rather stick to the truth as much as I can."

"I agree."

At Tory's apartment, Griffin knocked and then opened the door. Kenton was there, but Bevon wasn't.

"Good. You've come."

"Of course," Griffin said. "Where's Tory?"

"In her room. Just go in and gently shake her shoulder. When she wakes up, I imagine she'll be a little confused at first, but just tell her that it was your turn to watch her."

She stepped next to Kenton. "Can we tell her that you sent Malpan to some dark place?"

"I would rather you say he died."

"If Tory told you what happened, I trust she was awake in your realm."

Kenton inhaled, as if he needed some time to think how much to reveal. "Yes, for a little while. I would have returned her two days ago, but we wanted to be certain she was fully recovered."

Thankfully, Griffin seemed satisfied with his answer. Once more he held out his hand. "Thanks again."

"See you around."

With that, he disappeared. She turned to Griffin. "Okay, he is beginning to freak me out."

"Me, too. Let's go wake up Tory."

Chapter Twenty-Four

WHEN DANITA AND Griffin stepped into Tory's bedroom to wake her, Danita held her breath. His cousin looked so peaceful. Danita never would have guessed that she'd almost died.

Interestingly, she had on a clean T-shirt, but Danita had no idea if it was the same one she wore to the fight or not. Had someone on Feyrion given her a T-shirt? Or was this her own? If it was a fresh one, who had dressed her? Kenton? Now wasn't the time to ponder that interesting thought though.

Griffin stepped over to the bed, leaned over, and gently shook her shoulder. "Tory? Time to wake up." When she moaned, Griffin smiled. "That's it. Open your eyes."

Her lids lifted, and then she bolted upright, as if she were completely healthy—something that Kenton claimed was true.

"What are you guys doing here?" She looked down and then pulled up the blanket over her chest. Maybe she didn't have on a bra.

"You were injured in the fight. After you fell through the trees, Malpan found you and infected you with his dark magic."

Her eyes widen. "Is it still in me?"

Griffin smiled, looking so gentle. "No. You're cured."

Tory glanced off to the side. "How long have I been out?"

"Tell me what you remember," Griffin said not missing a beat.

"After I opened the door to the mine, I went around the one side just as you asked. I found an entrance and entered. A second later, I sensed other shifters and left. I thought I was doomed. I shifted just as Stone and Logan appeared. I was fighting one dragon until a second one showed up. Stone and Logan had their hands full at the time. The two dragons nudged me at just the wrong angle, and I went into a spin. I remember that my wings slowed down my fall. I think I was knocked out for a little bit, but then I remember getting up." She rubbed her forehead. "It's a bit fuzzy. I think Wendy was there."

Danita smiled. "Yes." She didn't want to say too much more. Mentioning Kenton would only cause too many questions. "She's safe and sound."

"So Malpan was behind all of this."

"Yes, and I am happy to say he is no longer of this realm."

"Good."

Griffin stood. "Since you seem to have healed, I promised Danita dinner at Highlanders'."

"That is so sweet." She made a shooing motion. "Go. Have a great time. I'll give Kaleena a call to let her know I'm okay."

"That's a good idea."

"We need to get out of here before I let something slip," he telepathed.

"No kidding." Being able to communicate this way was so cool.

Once outside, he strode toward the stairwell, making it hard to keep up. "Wait up," she called.

He slowed. "I'm sorry. Deceiving anyone goes against my grain, but we promised Kenton."

Danita rubbed his arm. "You didn't lie."

"Lying by omission is the same thing."

Danita planted a hand on her hip. "Griffin Caspian. What will it take for you to stop blaming yourself? I'm getting tired of it. Tory will be okay, and Logan is giving everyone the lowdown. Kenton's secret will be safe. It is better this way and you know it."

"You're right, but what will she think when she looks at the calendar and realizes she's been asleep for days?" He wrapped an arm around her waist and escorted her to the elevator.

He was being ridiculous. "She'll believe that her body needed time to heal from the dark magic. Remember, it took me five months to get better."

"You had help from Kenton."

"Tory had help too. Maybe she'll think she stepped in the path of some bad juju."

He chuckled. "Bad juju?"

"You know, some spell that went wrong. We all are aware that these men had some kind of spell put on them. She'll believe she had the same thing happen to her."

"You're probably right. Hell, after what we've seen with Fey dark magic and this other realm, nothing would surprise me." Griffin leaned over and kissed her. "You are good for me, Danita Warren."

"I know I am. You do know we'll have to tell her we've mated."

He winced. "Yes, but let's give her a few days."

"Deal."

They took the elevator to the bottom floor since Highlanders' Steakhouse was only a couple of blocks away.

Once they were seated, Griffin ordered a bottle of Campovino. "We need to celebrate," he said.

"I agree. We have a lot to be thankful for."

"We do. For starters, I think you should totally move in with me and get rid of your apartment."

Joy shot through her. Danita never liked her place. "On one condition."

His brow rose. "And what is that?"

"While your condo is amazing, I'd like to add my own touches to the place. It's a little masculine. And don't get me started about the lack of kitchen appliances. If I'm going to cook, I'll need some better items—like a big mixing bowl for starters."

"Deal." He grinned. "I was hoping you'd volunteer. Believe it or not, my abilities in the kitchen outshine my ability to decorate, and we both know my meal repertoire is very limited."

"It is indeed. I'm glad I can help out in that department."

Griffin reached across the table. "You add so much to my life in so many ways that I can't even count them."

Heat raced up her face. "Thank you, but keep that up and I might have to show you a good time tonight."

His eyes swirled teal, and she swore a talon poked out of his fingers before he placed his hands on his lap. "Okay, no more talk like that until we finish eating."

She grinned. "Deal."

GRIFFIN WASN'T SURE how he was able to get through dinner. His need built with every second he watched Danita. She was charming, funny, and oh so sexy. Her delicious scent, which was some kind of flowery blend, was driving his dragon crazy. Now that Tory was safe and sound, Malpan was more or less dead, and Danita and he had mated, Griffin only had one thing on his mind—making love with Danita over and over again.

They both had mentioned they'd like children, but Danita said she wanted to enjoy being with Griffin for a while before they tried, and he totally agreed.

Working hard not to appear as if he was in a hurry—which of course he was—he motioned to their server for the check. After an eternal wait, he finally paid. "Ready?" he asked her.

"Yes. I assume you want your dessert at home."

Griffin slid out of the booth and helped her out. He then wrapped a tight arm around her waist. "You have no idea." He leaned over. "Are you wearing any underwear under that dress?"

"You will have to check and find out," she whispered.

"Oh, I definitely will." Griffin slid his hand down her backside.

Danita giggled "Hey! You better not be checking it out right now, handy."

He winked. "Walk faster, woman," he said and then gave her a slap on the ass.

The trip to his condo seemed to take forever, but it helped calm him a bit. His dragon? Not so much.

The second they entered the condo, Griffin was convinced he'd explode. Just going from the front door to the bedroom would take too long, so he spun Danita around and kissed her. When she leaned into him and groaned, all restraint flew out the window. Her inner dragon must have woken up, because in a flash, she kicked off her shoes and tried to undo his zipper.

Her impatience spurred him on. It was as if they were in a race to see who could undress whom faster.

Griffin broke the kiss. Taking off his shoes required untying them. "Give me a sec." He bent down, removed then, and then slid his footwear across the floor so they wouldn't get in the way. "Now where were we?" he asked.

"I think you were trying to get me naked. At least I hoped that was your plan."

"You know me well, dragon lady."

"Dragon lady? Cute, but I'm not really one yet."

He was well aware of her hesitancy to fly, but he had a plan all cooked up for tomorrow to put her mind at ease. "Time will tell," was all he would say.

Not able to wait any longer, he lifted her dress over her head. Underneath revealed a true treasure. "Oh, you bad girl, you didn't have your panties on."

She smiled. "Is that a problem?"

"Hell no."

"Good. Now it's my turn."

Griffin understood how much she enjoyed taking off his clothes. "Be my guest."

Usually, Danita liked to take her time, teasing and tempting him as she did. This time, she lifted off the shirt without any fanfare, and then unzipped his slacks and tugged them down as fast and as hard as she could.

"Step out of them," she commanded.

"One of us is still overdressed," he said as soon as he was naked. As she reached behind her back to unhook her bra, he swatted away her hands. "As desperate as I am, I want to do this right."

It might kill him to wait, but for Danita's sake, he was willing to risk it. Pressing her against the sofa back, he unclasped her bra. His mouth watered in anticipation of sucking on her delicious tits. Moving as slowly as his dragon allowed, he lowered the straps on her pretty white bra. When her peachy brown nipples appeared, his teeth sharpened, and he flashed up a storm.

Griffin lifted her up and set her on top of the sofa, putting her closer to mouth height. He then pressed on one breast as he leaned over and suckled on her nipple. Danita reached out and grabbed his shoulders. Whoa. Her nails sure had sharpened. He might have mentioned it, but he didn't want to freak her out and say she was close to drawing blood. The added pain actually helped to slow him down. With deliberation, he licked, sucked, and teased the tiny nub into a peak.

"That feels so good," she panted. Danita lowered one hand and tried to grab his dick, but thankfully she couldn't reach it. If she had touched him, he would have been lost for sure.

Once he moved over to her other side, he couldn't take it much longer. Dropping to his knees, in front of her heated sex had his dragon clawing and begging for some hardcore loving.

Soon, he promised his animal.

I'm not a patient dragon.

No kidding. Determined to make this an amazing experience for her, Griffin widened her legs and licked her opening.

"Griffin!"

Her hands found his shoulders again, but she must have realized that her nails had become dangerous, because she didn't dig them into his skin—skin that had already started to harden into scales. He needed to hurry.

Desperate to bring her to climax, he slipped two fingers into her while he sucked on her clit. His wanton woman lasted a mere ten seconds before she yelled and then moaned. Her body sagged implying she was temporarily sated.

Griffin stood, slipped her off the sofa back and flipped her around. He then pressed on her back forcing her to plant her elbows on the seatback. Probably to drive him even crazier, she stuck out her hips. From her scented arousal, she was ready. And so was he. Stepping close behind her, he clasped her waist, and aimed. The first thrust was so divine that it almost caused him to come.

Danita lowered her head onto her wrists and wiggled her hips. He prayed: *Dear Fate, please let me last a little bit longer.*

Griffin didn't know what came over him, but he palmed her breasts, lightly pinching her nipples and then rubbing the tips across his palms. Wild spikes of need surged, and his lit scales nearly blinded him. Danita's glow also intensified, growing larger and larger with each thrust. He grunted as he plowed into her again and again.

It was time. He dipped his head and pressed his sharpened teeth against her delicate soft neck. As he bit her, his seed shot out. Danita's inner walls clamped down hard on him. She too let out a yell that didn't quite seem human.

Seconds later, she nearly dropped to her knees, but he kept her from falling by wrapping an arm around her waist. Pressing his face against the back of her head, he inhaled. "I love you, Danita Warren."

Her nod said it all. They would be together for a long time.

Chapter Twenty-Five

D ANITA AWOKE TO the sound of her phone. Keeping her eyes closed, she reached out and snagged it. Both she and Griffin had an amazing evening last night celebrating so many things, but the lovemaking kept going for much of the night. Now all she wanted to do was sleep.

Cracking open an eye, she realized it wasn't all that early. The phone kept ringing. When her eyes finally focused, she sat up. It was her old boss.

"Hello?"

"Danita, this is Bill Bradley."

"Thanks for getting back to me." From his cheery tone, he was willing to give her a letter of recommendation.

"I'm sorry I didn't call sooner, but I was waiting on some information first. I was thrilled to hear from you and so happy you are feeling better."

"Thank you. I am very happy to be back to my old self again." Bill would never understand just how accurate that statement was.

"Since your departure, we've had some turnover. You, Danita, are not replaceable. I'd love it if you would return to work here."

If she hadn't clamped a hand over her mouth, she might have screamed. "Thank you so much. I would love to."

"Can you start tomorrow?" he asked.

She had no other plans, other than to move out of her apartment. She supposed that since her lease wasn't up until the end of the month, moving could wait. "Absolutely."

"Great. See you then."

When he disconnected, she clasped the phone to her chest. She couldn't believe it. Her life had totally turned around, and she couldn't wait to tell Griffin. Danita jumped out of bed. If she hadn't been naked, she would have gone into the living room right then and there. Knowing Griffin, they'd be back in bed in a flash.

She tossed on some clothes, brushed her teeth, and washed her face. When she opened the bedroom door, the smell of eggs filled the room. "You're cooking?" she asked.

Griffin had a spatula in his hand and was wearing one of her aprons. Damn. She should grab her phone and take his picture. It would be a photo she'd frame.

He smiled. "Today is going to be a special day."

That's not what she'd expected him to say. "Really? Why?"

"It's a secret. Take a seat. I thought I'd have to wake you. I'm glad you are up."

"I figured you didn't come into the bedroom and wake me because you knew we'd end up making love."

He laughed. "So true. I figured you could use the sleep. Who was on the phone?"

The man did have good hearing. "That was my old boss, and guess what?"

"What?" he asked as he flipped over what smelled like eggs and cheese in the pan.

"He offered me my old job back. I start tomorrow."

Griffin rushed over and hugged her. "I'm so happy for you."

"Me, too." She nodded to the kitchen. "What can I do to help?"

He waved a hand and reentered the kitchen. "I got this."

True to his word, Griffin finished cooking the omelet with mushrooms, spinach, and cheese. He'd also made toast, which she admitted didn't require a lot of culinary talent, but nonetheless, she appreciated that he went to the trouble.

He placed their plates on the table and then poured them coffee. "Dig in."

From the joy in his voice, he was proud of his accomplishment.

On the first bite, she groaned. "This is really, really good. You might have to make breakfast every morning."

"Not going to happen, princess."

"So now I'm a princess?" Teasing him was always so much fun.

He picked up his cup and didn't gulp it down like he usually did, probably because it was still steaming hot. "I'm just saying, today is special."

Now he had her curious. "I know you'll tell me when the time is right."

"Actually, I will be showing you after we eat."

"I can't wait."

Because Griffin had cooked, she insisted on cleaning up while he showered and shaved. When he came out dressed in jeans and a long sleeve blue shirt, she almost debated delaying the surprise. He looked so fine.

"Ready?" he asked.

"Where are we going?"

"As I said, it's a surprise."

"Lead the way."

Once on the rooftop, he asked if she wanted to try shifting. It was a reasonable request. Danita had been debating it. "How about tomorrow?"

"No problem."

That was the first time he gave up so easily, and that almost scared her. "You aren't just going to drop me in midair and hope I take flight, are you?"

His cheer evaporated. He stepped close and clasped her shoulders. "I would never do that to you."

"Okay, okay. I just wanted to make sure."

Griffin stepped back, and once in his dragon form, he reached out his claw and she grabbed hold. A second later, they were soaring high. Oh, how she'd come to learn to love the skies. It was possible she didn't want to learn to fly, because she didn't want to give up being in his arms.

At first, she wasn't sure where they were headed, but soon she began to suspect they were going to her favorite spot—high in the hills where the wild flowers abound. Sure enough, once he landed in the middle of the field, he set her down and shifted.

While she loved being here, Danita wasn't totally sure what the surprise part was.

Griffin opened his arms. "What do you think?"

"About what? You know it's my favorite place in the world."

"That's why I bought this piece of land."

It took her a moment to understand. "You actually bought this place?"

"Yes, and much of the surrounding area. I want total privacy for when we are naked in our hot tub looking up at the evening stars."

This was too fantastic to imagine. "You want to live here?" Then she'd have to learn to fly if she planned to get to work on time.

"No. I thought we could enjoy it on the weekends and for vacations if we want. I've asked a contractor by the name of Slade LaMont to build us a small cabin."

She threw herself in his arms. "That is the most amazing gift in the world."

He leaned back and stroked her face. "No, you are the most amazing gift in the world."

She couldn't love him more if she tried. "Thank you." He turned her around to face the vista. Danita sighed. "I think I am ready to fly."

He spun her around. "By yourself?"

She grinned. "Yes. I want to try."

"I'll be right by your side in case you freak out."

Danita stroked his arm. "With you by my side, I'll be able to fly and do anything."

"Then let's do it!"

I hope you enjoyed reading Danita and Griffin's story as much as I enjoyed writing it.

Don't forget to sign up for my newsletter *to receive three free books, as well as up-to-date information on my stories. If you prefer to only receive notices regarding my releases, follow me on BookBub.*

http://smarturl.it/VellaDayNL

bookbub.com/authors/vella-day

Next up will be Wendy and Logan's story.

THE END

HIDDEN REALMS OF SILVER LAKE (Paranormal)

Awakened By Flames (book 1)

Seduced By Flames (book 2)

Kissed By Flames (book 3)

Destiny In Flames (book 4)

Passionate Flames (book 5)

Ignited By Flames (book 6)

Touched By Flames (book 7)

FOUR SISTERS OF FATE: HIDDEN REALMS OF SILVER LAKE (Paranormal)

Poppy (book 1)

Primrose (book 2)

Acacia (book 3)

Magnolia (book 4)

Box Set (books 1-4)

Jace (book 5)

WERES AND WITCHES OF SILVER LAKE (Paranormal)

A Magical Shift (book 1)

Catching Her Bear (book 2)

Surge of Magic (book 3)

The Bear's Forbidden Wolf (book 4)

Her Reluctant Bear (book 5)

Freeing His Tiger (book 6)

Protecting His Wolf (book 7)

Waking His Bear (book 8)

Melting Her Wolf's Heart (book 9)

Her Wolf's Guarded Heart (book 10)

His Rogue Bear (book 11)

Box Set (books 1-4)

Box Set (books 5-8)

Awakening Their Bears (book 12)

ROCK HARD, MONTANA (contemporary novellas)

Montana Desire (book 1)

Awakening Passions (book 2)

HIDDEN HILLS SHIFTERS (Paranormal)

An Unexpected Diversion (book 1)

Bare Instincts (book 2)

Shifting Destinies (book 3)

Embracing Fate (book 4)

Promises Unbroken (book 5)

Bare 'N Dirty (book 6)

Hidden Hills Shifters Complete Box Set (books 1-6)

Author Bio

Want three FREE books? Sign up for my newsletter and receive MONTANA DESIRE, AN UNEXPECTED DIVERSION, and BARE INSTINCTS.
COPY AND PASTE INTO YOUR BROWSER:
http://smarturl.it/o4cz93?IQid=MLite

Check out my latest interview on You Tube:
http://youtube/sQo5pyyVMDI

Not only do I love to read, write, and dream, I'm an extrovert. I enjoy being around people and am always trying to understand what makes them tick. Not only must my books have a happily ever after, I need characters I can relate to. My men are wonderful, dynamic, smart, strong, and the best lovers in the world (of course).

I believe I am the luckiest woman. I do what I love and I have a wonderful, supportive husband, who happens to be hot!

Fun facts about me

(1) I'm a math nerd who loves spreadsheets. Give me numbers and I'll find a pattern.
(2) I just moved to Costa Rica and live on the beach!
(3) I also like to exercise. Yes, I know I'm odd.

I love hearing from readers either on FB or via email (hint, hint).

Social Media Sites

Website:
www.velladay.com

FB:
facebook.com/vella.day.90

Twitter:
@velladay4

Gmail:
velladayauthor@gmail.com

Instagram:
@dayvella